STORIES FROM THE BIBLE

STORIES FROM THE BIBLE

By Elsie E. Egermeier

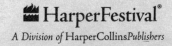
HarperFestival®

A Division of HarperCollinsPublishers

Stories from the Bible

HarperCollins®, ®, and HarperFestival®
are trademarks of HarperCollins Publishers, Inc.

Printed in the United States of America. All rights reserved.

www.harperchildrens.com

For information address HarperCollins Children's Books, a division of HarperCollins Publishers,

1350 Avenue of the Americas, New York, NY 10019

Library of Congress catalog card number: 2004107733

Typography by Tom Starace

1 2 3 4 5 6 7 8 9 10

❖

First HarperFestival edition, 2005

The LORD is my shepherd; I shall not want.

He maketh me to lie down in green pastures: he leadeth me
beside the still waters.

He restoreth my soul: he leadeth me in the paths of
righteousness for his name's sake.

Yea, though I walk through the valley of the shadow of death,
I will fear no evil: for thou art with me; thy rod and thy
staff they comfort me.

Thou preparest a table before me in the presence of mine
enemies: thou anointest my head with oil; my cup
runneth over.

Surely goodness and mercy shall follow me all the days of my
life: and I will dwell in the house of the LORD for ever.

—Psalm 23

CONTENTS

STORIES OF THE
OLD TESTAMENT

THE CREATION

Genesis 1:1–2:7

THIS GREAT WORLD IN WHICH WE LIVE did not always exist. The broad expanse of sky, which smiles upon us when days are fair, and frowns and weeps when days are foul, did not always form an arch above our earth. Long, long ago there was no world at all. There was no sun to shine, there were no stars to twinkle, nor moonbeams to play through the night shadows. But even then there was God; for he ever has been and always shall be the same unchanging Divine Being.

Then, away back at the very beginning of time, God made the world. Not as we see it today, for at first water covered everything, and all was darkness everywhere. What a strange, unfriendly world this must have been, for no living creature could dwell in it! But God planned to make it beautiful, so he caused the light to shine. This light he called Day and the darkness he called Night. And then the evening and morning of the first day of time passed by.

On the second day God made the beautiful blue sky, and placed above the water-covered earth clouds to carry the sky's moisture. He called the sky Heaven. On the third day he caused the waters to flow together in wide, deep places, and he called them Seas. Dry land then rose up, and this he called Earth. But as yet there were no grasses, flowers, or trees—the whole earth was barren and desolate. So God caused a carpet of grass to grow upon the bare ground and beautiful flowers to spring up from the earth. The trees and herbs also he made to grow at his will. When God beheld all these things he saw that they were good.

On the fourth day appeared the great lights that we see in the sky—the sun, the moon, and the stars. These he made to divide the day from the night.

On the fifth day, God began to create living creatures. He made fishes of all kinds and sizes to swim about in the seas and birds of every description to fly about above the water and land, just as we see them doing today. Thus the world continued to become more delightful, and the fifth day of the first week of time passed by.

On the sixth day God made all the animals, great and small, and every creeping thing. Then there was life abounding in the woods and on the plains, as well as in the air and in the sea. What a beautiful world! Still what a strange world, for there were no people in it! Not a home anywhere—not a man, woman, nor little child to be seen. What a very strange world indeed!

But God had not yet finished his work of creation, for

he wished to have people live in the wonderful world he had made. They could enjoy its beauties and take care of it as no other living creature could do. And more, they could know who had made all these great things, and knowing God they could love and worship him. So it was that God made the first man. Out of the dust of the ground he made the man's body, then he breathed into that body with the breath of life and man became alive—not just as the birds and the fishes and the animals were alive, for God gave to man a soul that would never die.

This first man God called Adam, and to Adam he gave the power to rule over all the other living creatures. These animals and birds he brought to Adam, and Adam gave each of them a name. But not one of them did Adam find suitable for a helper, and because he needed a helper very much God made for him a woman. This woman became Adam's wife, and he loved her very much. He called her name Eve.

When the sixth day ended God had made the world and had placed everything in it just as he wished, therefore on the seventh day he rested from his work.

Gen. 2:8—3:24

God himself made for Adam and Eve their first home. And a beautiful home it was. God chose a place from which four rivers flowed and there he planted a large garden. We do not know the many kinds of trees and flowers and vegetables and grasses that he caused to grow in this garden. But we are sure that no park that man has made could be so lovely as was the Garden of

Eden. In the midst of this garden God planted a wonderful tree, called the tree of life. Whoever might eat of the fruit of this tree would live on and on forever.

Adam and Eve were very happy. God had given them good things to enjoy, and they knew nothing about evil and wrong-doing. They often talked with God and listened to his voice as he walked and talked with them in the cool of evening time.

God wanted Adam and Eve to prove their love for him, and for this reason he planted in the beautiful garden one test-tree, called the tree of knowledge of good and evil. "Of the fruit of every other tree in this garden you may eat," God had told them, "but the fruit of this tree you must not taste. If you do, you shall surely die."

We do not know how long Adam and Eve enjoyed their beautiful garden home, but we do know that one day a sad thing happened. Sin crept slyly into this lovely place. It came first to Eve. She heard a voice and saw a snake talking to her. She was not afraid, because she had never known fear. So she listened. "Has God said that you must not eat the fruit of every tree in this garden?" the snake asked.

"We may eat of every tree except one," Eve answered. "God has told us that we must not eat of the tree of knowledge of good and evil, or else we will die."

"That is a mistake; you will not die," the snake replied. "God knows that if you eat fruit from this tree you will become wise to know good and evil, as he is wise, therefore he has forbidden you to eat of it."

Until this time Eve had not touched the forbidden tree;

but now she looked at its fruit and thought that if it really would make her wise like God, she wanted to taste it. Soon she yielded to the temptation and plucked the fruit, and then she gave some to Adam, and he too ate of it.

At once Adam and Eve knew what a dreadful thing sin is. They knew they had disobeyed God. A strange something stole into their hearts; it was fear. How afraid they were to meet God! They had never been afraid before, but now they tried to find a hiding place among the beautiful trees in the garden. Their hearts had become wicked.

Soon a voice called, "Adam, where are you?" and the frightened man answered, "Lord, I heard your voice and I was afraid, therefore I hid myself." "Why should you be afraid to meet me?" God asked. "Have you eaten of the forbidden fruit?" Then Adam told God that Eve had given him some of the fruit and he had eaten it.

"What is this you have done?" God questioned Eve. And she told him what the snake had said. "I listened to the tempter and then ate of the fruit and gave it to my husband," was her sorrowful confession.

God was grieved because Adam and Eve had failed to obey him. Now he knew they could no longer enjoy his presence with them, because sin had spoiled their lives. They were no longer fit to live in the beautiful garden he had made for them. So he sent them away out into the world to make a home for themselves. And he placed an angel at the gate of the garden to prevent them from coming back to eat of the fruit that grew on the wonderful tree of life.

To Eve, God said, "Because you listened to the tempter's

voice and disobeyed me, you shall have pain and trouble all the days of your life."

Adam also received a sentence of punishment from God. No longer should the ground yield freely of the fruits and vegetables that Adam and Eve ate for food; now Adam must work hard to keep these things growing. And he would find that weeds and thorns and thistles would grow in his fields to make his work even harder. Then by and by he would grow old and feeble, and then he would die and his body would again become dust as it was before God created him. All these sorrows came because of sin.

But while God drove Adam and Eve out of the beautiful garden, he at the same time gave them the promise that he would someday send a Savior to make all men free from sin and death.

Gen. 4

After sin caused God to shut Adam and Eve out of the beautiful garden that he had made for them, they built a home for themselves somewhere outside the garden gate. Here they began to feel more and more the punishment that their sin had brought upon them. Adam had to toil hard and long to secure food for himself and for Eve. No doubt his hands and feet were sometimes bruised and torn by thistles and thorns. Eve too learned the sad meaning of pain and sorrow. Her home was not so happy as it had been before she listened to the tempter's voice, and chose to disobey God.

But all the while God loved Adam and Eve. We cannot

know how great was his grief when they sinned. No longer could he walk and talk with them as he had done before. Now sin, like a great, black monster, had stepped in and spoiled their friendship, and where sin dwells God will not go. No doubt Adam and Eve were sorry, too. No longer could they have God's presence in their home because sin had fastened itself in their hearts.

But because God loved them still, he gave Adam and Eve a promise of a Savior. And because they believed the promise, hope came into their hearts again. Although they could not talk to God as they had done in their garden, now they confessed their sins to him.

We are sure that Adam and Eve must have felt lonely, with no friends in all the big, wide world. But God planned that there should be more people, and so one day he gave Adam and Eve a little child—a baby boy. This baby they named Cain. How they must have loved him! After a while God gave them another little boy, and they named him Abel.

When Cain and his little brother Abel grew old enough to understand, Adam and Eve told them about the great God, and how they themselves had disobeyed him before Cain and Abel were born. They wanted their sons to love this God and try to please him. But alas! sin, like a tiny seed, was already buried in the hearts of these little boys, causing them to think naughty thoughts, or say unkind words, or do wrong deeds, just as little boys and girls are tempted to do today. Abel wanted to please God and he was sorry because he sinned; but Cain allowed the tiny sin-seed to grow and grow until his heart became very wicked.

By and by Cain and Abel became men, like Adam, and

Cain worked in the fields raising grain and fruits, while Abel took care of a flock of sheep. These brothers built altars, upon which they offered their gifts to God, as their parents did. Cain brought for his offering fruit from the field where he had labored, and Abel brought a fat lamb. But Cain's offering did not please God. When he saw that God was displeased, he became very angry. God talked to him. He warned him of the harm that might come if he should continue to be angry instead of becoming sorry for his sins. But Cain was not willing to listen; he was not sorry for his sins.

Abel believed the promise that God had given to his parents, and when he offered his gift he prayed and asked God to forgive his sins. God was pleased with Abel's offering.

One day while the brothers were together in the field, Cain quarreled with Abel. Now, we are sure that nothing good can come of quarrels, because they are so wrong. This quarrel ended dreadfully. Cain grew so angry with Abel that he killed him. What an awful deed!

God spoke again to Cain, and asked, "Where is Abel your brother?"

Cain replied, "I know not. Am I my brother's keeper?"

Wicked Cain did not know that God had seen all he did. And now for a punishment God told Cain that he must go farther away out into the wide world. Never again should he know the blessing of his old home, for hereafter he should wander about from place to place like a frightened, hunted animal. He should have a terrible fear in his heart always that some one would kill him as he had killed his brother.

Now at last Cain felt sorry, but he was sorry only because he was to be punished for his sin. He thought God was punishing him more than he could bear. Then God placed a mark upon him that all could see, and by that mark they would know that God did not want them to kill Cain.

After this Cain wandered far away into a land called Nod. There he lived for many long years.

Adam and Eve lived a long time, and God gave them other children besides Cain and Abel. Then the time came at last when their bodies grew feeble with age and they died, as God had said they should when they ate the forbidden fruit.

Gen. 5:1–9:17

The children of Adam and Eve lived to be very old. Their children also lived for several hundreds of years. And so it was that grandsons became grandfathers before their own grandfathers died. Thus several generations lived and worked together. After a while there were many people living in the world.

We do not know very much about those people of long ago except the fact that many of them were very wicked. Among them was one man, however, who, like Abel, tried to please God. This man's name was Enoch. The Bible tells us that Enoch walked with God. We understand that he loved God better than he loved anything else, and talked to God and listened when God talked to him. Finally Enoch became an old man. At last, when he was three hundred and sixty-five years old, one day God took him away from earth to heaven, and he did not die. Enoch had a son whom he named Methuselah. This man lived for nine hundred and sixty-nine years, until he was older than any other man had ever been. Then he died, like all other people had done except his father Enoch.

By this time there were many, many people living in the world. And their hearts were so full of sin that their thoughts and words and deeds were all very wicked. They did not try to please God at all. They did not love him. They did not thank him for the blessings of food and shelter and sunshine that he gave to them. They did not teach their children to love good, pure things, but allowed them to grow up and become evil men and women like themselves. What a sad world this was, for sin was everywhere.

Finally God planned to destroy all the people because they were no longer fit to live. He felt sorry that he ever had made man. He thought he would destroy everything—people, animals, and every other creature that lived on the earth. He would cause a great flood of water to cover the earth.

Then God remembered Noah. Here was a man who had tried to do right regardless of all his wicked surroundings. And he had taught his sons to do right also. God was pleased with Noah and with his sons. Sometimes he talked to Noah. Now he told him about his plan to destroy the world. But because Noah and his family had been trying to do right and trust in the Lord, God promised that they should not be destroyed with the wicked people.

"Get ready to build an ark," God told Noah, "and then when it is finished you and your wife, your sons and their wives may go into this ark and live there until the flood is ended."

Now that God decided to save a few people he also

arranged to save a pair of each kind of animal and bird and of every living thing on the earth that breathed. These creatures were to be housed in the ark, too, while the flood should last.

Noah believed God and made ready to build the ark. God had told him how it should be built. For a long time, while others went their wicked way, he and his sons worked, sawing boards and hammering nails, and making every part of the ark just exactly as God had said it should be made. Then by and by every nail was driven securely into its place, the inside walls were finished, and every part was ready for the purpose it should serve. What a queer-looking building now stood before them—a very large boatlike house three stories high, away out on dry land! Doubtless the people laughed much at faithful old Noah and his three sons. Perhaps they thought that only gullible folk could believe that there ever would be such a thing as a flood. Still Noah continued to warn them that they should repent of their sins lest God destroy them.

One day, when the ark was completed and everything else was in readiness, God called Noah and told him to bring his wife, his three sons and their wives, and come into the ark. And the animals and birds and creeping things God caused to come also, two of every kind; and of those animals which man should need after the flood, and birds, seven pairs of each kind came. When they were all inside the ark, God himself shut the door.

After a few days the rain began to fall. And such a rain! Great sheets of water poured down from the clouds as if windows in the sky had been opened and water was flowing through them. Soon the tiny streamlets were raging torrents and the rivers were overflowing their banks. People began to forsake their homes and rush to the hills for safety. Animals, too, ran everywhere, trying to find a place of refuge and shelter from the storm. But still it rained, and higher and higher the waters rose until everyone believed at last that Noah had told the truth. But now it was too late to repent and seek refuge in the ark, for God had shut the door. And so when the waters crept up to the tops of the hills and mountains and finally buried them out of sight, every living creature on the face of the earth was drowned. Those in the ark were the only ones left alive.

For forty days and nights the downpour of rain continued; but Noah and his family were safe. When the waters rose high enough they lifted the ark off the ground, and it began to float about like a great ship on the top of the flood. For six months and more it floated high above the water-covered earth. Then one day it came to a standstill. God had caused a wind to blow over the waters to dry them up, and as the flood-tide became gradually lower, the ark had found a lodging-place on the top of a mountain. Here it rested for two months, and all the while the watermark continued to drop lower down the mountainsides.

After waiting for some time, Noah opened a window, which must have been very high up, near the roof. He allowed a bird called a raven to fly out of the window. Now, the raven has strong wings, and this bird flew to and fro until the waters had gone down. After some days, Noah sent out a dove; but this bird could not find a place to build her nest, so she soon returned again to the ark. Another week of waiting passed, and Noah sent the dove out once more. She stayed longer this time; and when evening came she flew back to Noah, bringing a green olive-leaf in her mouth. At this Noah and his family knew that the waters were returning to the rivers and the seas, and that the land again was becoming green and beautiful. One more week they waited, and now when Noah sent out the dove she flew away and never returned.

Now Noah believed that the time had come when he might uncover the roof and look out upon the earth. How glad he must have been to see dry land again; for more than a year had passed since God had shut them inside the ark. And God said to him, "Come out of the ark, with your wife and your sons and their wives, and every living thing that is with you in the ark." So Noah opened the great door, and he and his family stepped out upon the dry ground. All the animals and the birds and the creeping things came out also, and began to live upon the earth as they had done before the flood.

Noah was thankful to God because his life and the lives of his family had been saved when all other people had perished from off the earth. He built an altar as soon as he came out of the ark, and brought his offering to God. Because Noah had been obedient, God accepted his offering and was pleased with his household.

God then promised that never again would he send another flood to destroy every living creature, and that as long as the earth should remain there would be summer and winter, springtime and autumn, and day and night. And because God wanted mankind to remember always the promise that he would never again destroy the earth with a flood, he placed in the sky a sign of his promise. That sign was a beautiful rainbow. Have you ever seen that rainbow-sign? It is God's promise to all mankind—to you and to me as well as to Noah and his children.

Gen. 9:18–11:9

A clean, new world lay before Noah and his three sons when they stepped out of the ark. Now there were no wicked neighbors to mock them when they built altars to worship God. Even the wicked works of those wicked people had been swept away out of sight. Everything was ready for a new beginning.

Noah and his sons set to work and made new homes. Noah's sons were named Shem, Ham, and Japheth. After a while God gave them children. These children grew up and made homes for themselves. Then there were other children; and so it came about that the number of people grew and grew until the earth became as full of people as it was before the flood.

From the mountain of Ararat, where the ark lodged when the waters went down, the human family went into the south country. Later they moved east, into the valley of Mesopotamia, and there they lived on a plain in the land of Shinar.

"Let us build for ourselves a city," said the people some time after they reached Shinar, "and let us make a tower so great and high that its top will reach up to the sky. Then we shall not be scattered over the face of the earth, and separated from one another." And so the people set to work.

In this land of Shinar the soil is such that bricks can be made of it, and soon many bricks were made and ready for use. What a busy people! Some were making brick, others were mixing mortar, and still others were carrying brick and mortar to the workmen who were building the city and the tower. Everything was moving fast and everybody was thinking that some day their city and their wonderful tower would be finished.

Then something happened that the people had not expected to happen at all. God came to see the city and the tower. He did not talk to the builders, and very likely they did not know he had been there to look upon their work. But God was not pleased with what he saw. He knew that men would become more sinful if they should finish that great tower. Already they were thinking more and more about their own work and less and less about the God who gave them strength with which to labor. Soon they might forget God entirely and worship the work their own hands had made. So God planned to stop their building.

Until this time all the people in the world spoke one language. Now God caused them to speak different languages. The people of one family could not understand what their neighbors were talking about. Neither could their neighbors understand what they were saying. Such a great change caused the people to become restless, and all those who spoke one language moved into neighborhoods by themselves. They could no longer go on with their great building, either, because the workmen could not understand one another's language; and so at last they quit trying to finish the tower whose top they had planned should reach the sky. And the name of the city was called Babel.

Soon the people of one language gathered together their possessions and moved away from Babel. Others did the same. Across the plains they journeyed and over the mountains into strange lands where men's feet had never walked before. They built cities and planted fields and vineyards, and their numbers grew until they became strong nations.

THE STORY OF ABRAHAM AND ISAAC

Gen. 11: 27—12: 20

The people who moved away from Babel into different parts of the world did not pray to God. Their hearts were sinful, and they shrank away from the purity of God, like Adam and Eve did when they tried to hide from God's presence in the Garden of Eden. But we find that the people prayed to something. In every country where they went they had some kind of worship. Many of them worshiped things that God had made, such as the sun, the moon, and the stars. Afterward they also worshiped rivers and mountains and hills. They made images of wood and of stone to these things that they worshiped, and called the images gods. And so there was the sun-god, which they called Sham-ash, and the moon-god, which they called Ur, besides many others.

Not far from the city of Babel, where the tower was left unfinished, another city was built. This city was called Ur of the Chaldees, because it was built in the home country of the Chaldean people. These people worshiped the moon-god, Ur, and when they built their great city they named it in honor of their god. And so the moon-god became famous and was worshiped by the Chaldeans everywhere.

On the plains near Ur lived an old man who was a shepherd-farmer, that is, he tilled the soil and also raised large flocks of sheep and herds of cattle. His name was Terah. He had three grown sons, and their names were Abram, Nahor, and Haran. They were also shepherd-farmers. Haran did not live to be very old. When he died he left a son named Lot.

Now, Abram the son of Terah was a good man. He did not worship the moon-god as did his neighbors and friends and kinsfolk. He believed in the true God. He built altars and brought offerings to sacrifice to God just as Abel and Noah had done long years before. And his offerings pleased God, and his prayers were heard.

One day Abram heard the voice of God calling to him. He listened. God told him to gather together his family and his flocks and herds, bid farewell to his neighbors and friends, and start out on a long journey. God promised to lead him to a land far away, where he would bless him and make his name great. His children and their children in the generations to come God promised to bless, and to make into a great nation. And through them God promised to give a blessing to all families in the world.

Perhaps Abram did not understand the meaning of all

God's promise. He did not know that in the years to come a Savior should be born among the people of his own family, who would then be called the Jews. This Savior, we know, is the blessing that God promised to give to all families in the world, if Abram would obey his voice.

Although Abram did not know these things, nor even the country to which God wished to lead him, he was not afraid to go. So he took all his family—his wife, whose name was Sarai, his aged father, Terah, his brother Nahor and his wife, and the young son of his dead brother Haran. They and their servants Abram urged to start out with him on his journey. And they took all their possessions too—the tents in which they lived, and the large flocks of sheep and herds of cattle.

Day after day they journeyed up the great River Euphrates until they came to a place called Haran. Here they stopped to rest, and here Abram's aged father died and was buried. Even before that God spoke to Abram and urged him to continue his journey. But Nahor, Abram's brother, was unwilling to go farther, so he remained at Haran and made his home at that place.

After this Abram made a second start. Now he took only his wife, Sarai, his nephew Lot, and their servants. Driving their flocks and herds before them, they turned away from the great river and journeyed southwest, toward the land of Canaan. On one side of them the mountains rose wild and high, while on the other side, as far as they could see, the barren desert stretched away toward the south. On and on they traveled—across rivers, through valleys, over hills—each day farther from their homeland and nearer to the land that God had promised. We do not know how many days and weeks and months passed by before they came to the plain of Moreh, where God spoke again to Abram. "This is the land," God told him, "that I will give to you and to your children." And Abram built an altar there and worshiped God.

Now, this land of promise was called Canaan, because the Canaanite people lived in it. These people had been there for a long time and had built some towns and cities. Abram did not live among the Canaanite people, but pitched his tents out on the hills or plains, wherever he could find grass for his cattle and sheep to eat and water for them to drink. All the while his flocks and herds grew larger, until finally Abram became very rich.

Then there came a famine in the land. The grass failed and the waters of the brooks dried up. Nowhere could Abram find pasture, so he moved away from Canaan into the country called Egypt. Here he saw the great River Nile, and possibly even the pyramids and the sphinx. But he did not remain long in Egypt, because God did not want him to dwell there. When the famine ended in Canaan, he returned again to that country.

Gen. 13

After Abram returned from Egypt, he and Lot journeyed to the place where they had first pitched their tents in Canaan. There Abram had built an altar to worship God. At the very same place he now sacrificed another offering, and again talked to God.

Abram was now a very rich man. Not only did he possess many servants, flocks, and herds, but he also possessed much silver and gold. And we find that his nephew Lot owned many servants and sheep and cattle, too. Wherever these men and their servants pitched their tents, the place looked like a tent-town. And the country all around them would be dotted with cattle and sheep.

After some time trouble arose between the servants of Abram and Lot. Some of Abram's servants were caretakers of his cattle and sheep. They and the servants who cared for Lot's flocks quarreled. Abram's servants wanted the best pasture-land for Abram's flocks, and Lot's servants wanted that same land for their master's flocks. And so the trouble grew. By and by news of the quarrel reached the ears of Abram. He looked out over the crowded country and saw how hard it must be for the servants. How could they always find places nearby where tender grasses grew and where water was plentiful! He saw, too, the villages of the Canaanites not far away, and he knew there was not room enough in that part of the country for all to dwell together peaceably.

So Abram called Lot and said, "Let there be no quarrel between us, or between our servants. There is not room enough for both of us to dwell together with our flocks and herds. But see, the whole land lies before us. Let us separate. If you choose to go to the west country, then I shall journey east; but if you desire the east country, then I shall go west."

From the height upon which Abram and Lot stood to view the country they could see far to the east and to the west. Because Abram was the one to whom God had promised all this land, he could have chosen the better part, or he could have sent Lot and his servants away out of the land altogether. But Abram was not selfish. He kindly offered Lot the first choice. And Lot, forgetting the kindness of his uncle, thought only of his own interests and chose the east country, through which the Jordan River flowed. "I can always find plenty of grass and water there," he reasoned, "and my flocks and herds will grow in number until soon I shall become very rich, too."

After Lot departed with his possessions, God spoke again to Abram. Perhaps God saw that Abram felt lonely. So he comforted him by reminding him of the promise that the whole of Canaan's land should belong to him and to his children. As yet Abram and Sarai had no children, but God said that some day the children of their grandsons and great-grandsons should be many. And Abram believed God. God also told Abram to journey through the length and breadth of Canaan's land to see how large a country it was. So Abram moved away from the place where he and Lot had lived together for the last time, and came to a plain called Mamre. Here he pitched his tents under the oak trees near the city of Hebron, and then built another altar to worship God.

Gen. 14

When Lot selected the fertile plains of Jordan for his share of Canaan's land, he thought he was making a wise choice. He saw in the distance the large cities of the plain, called Sodom and Gomorrah. He knew that in those cities he could sell sheep and cattle from his flocks and herds, and soon have much silver and gold. So he moved toward Sodom. After a while he pitched his tents still nearer the city walls, and finally he moved his family inside the gate.

Now, Sodom was not a nice place for good people to live. The people of Sodom cared nothing about God. Some of them were very rich, and perhaps they had beautiful homes. But they had unlovely hearts. The Bible tells us that the men of Sodom were wicked and great sinners in God's sight. But in Lot's sight they were rich men, and clever, and so he brought his family to dwell among them. This was a sad mistake.

One day trouble came upon Sodom. There had been war in the land and the kings of Sodom, Gomorrah, and three other cities had gone out to battle. The army against which they fought defeated them. Then the conquering soldiers entered the gates of Sodom and of Gomorrah, crowded through the streets, and pushed their way into rich men's houses, taking everything that they could find to carry away. They even took people and led them away to become slaves. And Lot with his wife and children were taken with the others.

One of the captured men escaped and fled across the country to the place near Hebron where Abram lived. He told about the battle and what had happened to Lot. When Abram heard of Lot's trouble, he took three hundred and eighteen of his men servants and, with some friends, hurried in pursuit of the captives. After a long, hard march across the country they came upon the enemy's camp at a place in the north of Canaan, called Dan. It was night, and the unsus-pecting enemies lay asleep. Abram and his men rushed upon them and frightened them. They thought a great army had come to fight against them, and they were not prepared for a battle. So they rose up in haste and ran away, leaving behind their tents and all the goods and the people whom they had taken away from Sodom and Gomorrah.

This was a great victory for Abram. The people of Canaan honored him for his courage, and the king of Sodom went out to meet him. He offered Abram all the gold and silver and food and clothing that he had taken away from the enemy's camp, and asked only that the people be returned again to Sodom. But Abram would not accept any reward from the king, because he had promised God that he would not keep anything for himself. And so all the people and their possessions were again returned to their homes.

Another king also came out to meet Abram. His name was Melchisedec, and he was king of Salem, a place that was later called Jerusalem. Melchisedec was different from the other people of Canaan because he loved the true God and worshiped him. He was a priest of God. When this king met Abram he brought food for him, and then he asked God to bless Abram. He also thanked God for giving Abram such a great victory.

Because Melchisedec was a priest of the true God, Abram gave him a tenth of all the goods he had taken from the enemy's camp.

After this experience, Lot took his wife and children and went back again to live in wicked Sodom; but Abram returned to his quiet tent under the oak trees near Hebron.

Gen. 15–17

Abram was now growing old. Although he had great riches and many servants, he had no children. One night while he lay asleep in his tent, God appeared to him in a vision. "Do not be afraid," God told him, "for I will protect you, and will give you a great reward because you are faithful."

"What will you give me for a reward?" Abram asked. And God answered that some day Abram should have a son. Then, at God's bidding, Abram rose up and went outside his tent door and looked up at the starlit heavens. "The children of your family," God told Abram, "shall some day be as many as the stars—so many that no one can count them." Abram understood by this that God was speaking of the people who should some day possess Canaan's land, for they should be Abram's descendants. And he believed in the Lord, although he could not see even the beginning of that great family of promise.

God also caused Abram to understand that there would be a time when the children of his family should become slaves in a strange land, and should dwell there for four hundred years. After that they should again return to Canaan, and possess the land for their own. We shall see in later stories how this came to pass.

We remember that at one time Abram and his household journeyed into Egypt, during a famine in the land of Canaan. When they returned to Canaan they brought with them an Egyptian servant-girl named Hagar. They taught Hagar to know about the true God and to listen if he should speak to her. And they expected her to work faithfully for them.

One day Hagar did not please her mistress, Sarai. This was wrong, and Sarai punished her severely. Hagar became very unhappy, until finally she decided to run away.

Now, running away is never an easy thing to do, and as Hagar hastened along the sandy, desert road she grew very tired. So she stopped to rest by a fountain of water along the roadside. In this lonely place, in the deep wilderness, someone found her. It was an angel of the Lord.

"Hagar, Sarai's maid, where did you come from? and where are you going?" the angel inquired.

"I am fleeing from my mistress," Hagar replied, "because I am unhappy."

"Return again," the angel said, "and try to please Sarai. After a while God will give you a little son. He shall grow up to be a strong man, and he shall be called Ishmael."

Hagar knew it was a messenger from God who spoke to her. And she knew now that she could never run away from God, because he had seen her all the while. So she obeyed the angel's word and returned again to her mistress. Afterward that fountain of water in the wilderness where the angel found her was called Beer-lahai-roi, a word which means, "A well of the Living One who sees me."

So after Hagar returned to Sarai's tent-home, God gave her the child he had promised. Abram named him Ishmael, which means, "God hears." And Hagar remembered that this was the name by which the angel had said the child should be called. Abram loved Ishmael; but Ishmael was not the child that God had promised to give to him. We shall learn more about Hagar and Ishmael by and by.

The years passed on until Abram was nearly one hundred years old. Then God spoke to him again. Abram fell on his face and listened. God said, "I will make a covenant with you." Now, a covenant is a promise between two persons, each one agreeing to do something for the other. In this covenant God promised to give Abram a son and Abram promised to serve God faithfully. Then God said, "Your name shall no more be called Abram, but Abraham, which means, 'The father of many,' and your wife, Sarai, shall be called 'Sarah,' which means, 'Princess.'"

Gen. 18

It was noonday, and everywhere the sun shone hot upon the plains. But Abraham sat in the cool shade of his tent door, beneath a tree. Presently three strange men drew near. They did not look like other men, and Abraham knew they were from a far country. He hurried out to meet them, and, bowing low toward the ground just as he always did when greeting a friend or a visitor, he urged them to rest for a while in the cool shade. This they were quite ready to do.

Now we shall see how Abraham entertained his guests. First he sent for water to wash their feet. This was not unusual because people wore sandals in that long-ago time and it was customary for them to remove their sandals and wash their feet whenever they sat down to rest and visit. Next, Abraham told his wife to make ready and bake some barley cakes upon the hearth, while he should prepare some meat, for his guests. Then he ran out to his herd and selected a young calf, which he gave to a servant to dress and cook. When all was ready, he brought the food to his guests, and they ate while he stood under a tree nearby. Abraham was glad to serve these strangers because he was kind to every one.

When the meal was ended, the men arose to continue their journey. Abraham walked with them for a little way. By this time he knew they were not like other men, but they were heavenly beings. Two of them were angels. The other one was the Lord. And Abraham felt that he was unworthy to entertain such wonderful visitors. But because he was a good man the Lord loved him.

"Shall I hide from Abraham this thing which I do?" the Lord asked his companions. "I know that he will teach his children to keep my ways and to do right."

Then, turning toward Abraham the Lord said, "I am going to visit Sodom and Gomorrah to see if these cities are as wicked as they seem, for the cry of their sins has reached me."

The two men hurried on; but Abraham detained the Lord a while longer, because he wanted to talk to him. He knew the Lord would destroy the cities if he found them to be as wicked as they seemed, and he thought of Lot. Now, we remember that Lot had gone back to live again in Sodom after Abraham and his servants had rescued him and his family from the enemy's camp. Abraham knew that Lot too might perish if the cities should be destroyed. And he loved Lot. He wished once more to try to save him, so he said, "Will you destroy the righteous persons in the city, will you not spare the lives of all for their sake?" And the Lord promised to spare Sodom if he could find fifty righteous persons in it.

Abraham feared that there might be less than fifty. And he was troubled for Lot's safety. So he spoke again. "I know that I am but a common man, made of dust," said he, "yet I speak to the Lord. If there should be only forty-five righteous persons living in Sodom, will you spare the city?" And the Lord said he would spare Sodom for the sake of only forty-five righteous persons.

Still Abraham felt troubled. He feared there might not be even forty-five. So he asked if the city might be spared for the sake of forty. The Lord knew it was Abraham's love for the people that caused him to plead so earnestly for Sodom, and he promised to spare the city for the sake of forty.

"What," thought poor, distressed Abraham, "if there should not be even forty righteous persons found in Sodom?" And once more he spoke. "O Lord, be not angry with me," he said, "but if there are only thirty righteous persons, will you spare the city for their sakes?" And the Lord promised to spare the entire city if only thirty righteous people could be found in it. Abraham continued to plead until he had asked the Lord if he would spare the city if only ten righteous persons were found, and the Lord promised to spare Sodom if he could find only ten. Then the Lord passed on, and Abraham returned to his tent.

Gen. 19

The long shadows of evening-time were stealing over the hills and through the valleys, and everywhere people were hurrying toward home. Soon the city gates would be closed, and the wise men who sat there during the daytime to judge the people would be turning homeward, too.

Among the wise men who sat in Sodom's gate was Lot. On this evening he saw two strangers approaching, and he greeted them with a low bow, just as Abraham had greeted these same men earlier in the day. For they were no other than the angels who had dined with the Lord at Abraham's tent. Lot invited them to his home to spend the night, but they said they would stay out in the streets. Now, Lot knew the wicked men of Sodom would try to harm them if they remained in the streets, so he urged them to come with him. Finally they consented.

Here again the angels were entertained with hospitality, which may have reminded them of Abraham's kindness, for Lot brought water to wash their dusty feet and prepared good things for them to eat. Possibly Lot did not yet know that they were heavenly beings; but he thought they were strangers unlike the wicked men who lived in that city.

Soon the news spread all over Sodom that Lot had two strange-looking visitors at his home, and men came hurrying from every part of the city to see them. They planned to hurt them. But when Lot refused to let them see his guests, they pushed him aside and tried to break open the door. At this the angels drew Lot quickly inside, and then smote the men with blindness.

Now Lot knew that his visitors were angels, and that they had come to destroy Sodom because it was such a wicked place. He went out to the homes of his sons-in-law, two men of Sodom, and told them that the Lord was going to destroy their city. But they would not believe his words. And they would not listen when he told them to hurry and escape for their lives. So the night passed by.

When the early morning came, before the sun lightened the earth, the angels urged Lot and his wife and their two daughters to make haste and flee out of the city lest they also be destroyed. How hard it seemed for Lot to leave his home and his riches to be destroyed! But God was merciful to him, and the angels seized him and his family and dragged them outside the city. Then they bade them flee to the mountains for their lives, and not even pause long enough to take a backward glance toward their old home, because God would soon destroy the cities of that rich valley, and unless they hurried away they too should perish. But Lot's wife did not obey the angel's words. She looked back, and her body became changed into a pillar of salt.

Poor, unhappy Lot! Fear now tormented him from every direction. He thought his life would not be safe even in the mountains, for wild animals might devour him there. So he prayed to God to spare a small city nearby and allow him and his daughters to enter that place. God heard his prayer and granted his request, so they fled into that city. That place was called Zoar, which means little.

Just as the sun rose, Lot and his daughters entered the

gate of Zoar, and at that time God sent a great rain of fire and brimstone upon Sodom and Gomorrah and all the neighboring cities. So terrible was the fire that it completely destroyed the cities and all the wicked people nearby. Lot and his daughters feared that their lives were not safe in Zoar, so they hurried to the mountains, where God had first told them to go. There they made their home in a cave, far away from other people. After this time we hear no more about Lot, the man whose home and riches were destroyed because he chose to live among wicked people who hated God.

Gen. 20—21:21

After the destruction of Sodom and the other cities of the plain, Abraham moved away from Hebron. He journeyed south and west, into the land of the Philistines, near the Great Sea and made his home in a place called Gerar. Here he lived only a short time when God gave to him and Sarah the child of promise. Abraham named the child Isaac (a word meaning, in his language, "laughing") because both he and Sarah had laughed when God told them that they should have a son in their old age.

When the baby Isaac grew old enough to toddle about his home, and to lisp words, his father Abraham made a great feast for him. Perhaps many friends were invited, and every one knew that Isaac's parents thought he was a very wonderful little boy indeed. Before the day passed, however, something happened which brought sadness to the kind heart of Abraham.

You remember that Ishmael, the son of Hagar, Sarah's maid, also lived in Abraham's tent. These two boys, Ishmael and Isaac, may have played together sometimes, although Ishmael was much older than Abraham's little son. On this feast-day, when everybody else was happy, Ishmael was unkind to Isaac. Perhaps he felt jealous of the honor that Isaac was receiving from so many people.

When Sarah heard how unkindly Ishmael had treated her little boy she became angry, and called Abraham. "You must send Ishmael and his mother away," she told him, "for I do not want our little boy to grow up with such a rude companion." Now, Abraham loved Ishmael, too, and he felt sad to hear that the boy had mistreated his son. He thought that Ishmael might learn to be kind; but God told him to send the boy and his mother away, just as Sarah had said.

So the next morning Abraham called Hagar and told her that she must take Ishmael and go away. He gave her food for the journey and placed upon her shoulder a bottle filled with water. This bottle was not made of glass, but of the skin of an animal; for people used skin bottles in that long-ago time. Then Abraham bade them good-bye, and perhaps he watched them as they started toward the land of Egypt, where Hagar used to live when she was a little girl.

The road to Egypt led through the same desert where the angel spoke to Hagar when she had run away from Sarah's tent. On this second journey Hagar missed the road and wandered off into the trackless wilderness. She did not know which way to take; and after a while there was no more food in her basket nor water in the bottle that Abraham had given. And the hot sun beamed down upon the dry, burning sand all day, until Hagar and Ishmael grew so thirsty, faint, and weak that they could go no farther. Then Hagar laid her suffering boy beneath the shade of a little bush, and went away. "I can not bear to see him suffer and die," she said, and then she wept.

But God had not forgotten about Hagar and her boy. Just as he had seen her on her first journey into the wilderness, so he could see her now as she sat weeping all alone. And soon she heard a voice calling to her out of heaven, "What is the cause of your sorrow, Hagar? Do not be afraid, for God has heard Ishmael's cry of pain, and he will save his life and make of him a great nation. Go, now, and lift him up." Then Hagar saw a spring of water that God caused to bubble out of the dry ground nearby, and she quickly filled her empty bottle and gave Ishmael a drink.

After this Hagar and Ishmael did not journey on to Egypt, but made their home in the wilderness, far from other people. God cared for them, and Ishmael grew to be a strong, wild man. He became a hunter, and used a bow and arrow. His children also grew up in the wilderness, and were wild and strong like their father. They finally were called Arabians, and even today their descendants live in the desert and wander about wherever they please, just as Ishmael, their forefather, did so long ago.

t is God's will that people show their love for him by what they do. You remember how God wished to have the first man and woman show their love for him. He planted in their garden a test tree, the fruit of which he commanded them not to eat. And you remember also how they failed to obey his command, and so failed to show their love.

Abraham always listened to God's voice and obeyed. He left his own people and his homeland to journey into a country that he did not know, because God called him. And in our last story he sent Ishmael and Hagar away because God told him to do as Sarah had said. Even when it did not seem easy to obey, Abraham was always ready to do God's bidding.

After the baby Isaac came into Abraham's life, God saw that Abraham's love for the little boy was very strong. And the passing years increased this love, because Abraham knew that Isaac was the child God had promised, and he loved Isaac as a gift from God. He looked forward to the time when Isaac should become a man and should have children also, and he knew that these children should grow up and become the fathers of more people, because God had told him these things. And so whenever he looked upon Isaac and thought about these things, he knew that in this child were bound up all the promises of God for the coming years.

By and by the time came when Isaac grew far away from babyhood into youth. Abraham had taught him to know about God and to worship him. Perhaps he had taken Isaac with him when he offered gifts upon the altar, and he had told Isaac that God would accept the gifts and hear his prayers if he would try to do right. And Isaac loved his father Abraham, and was obedient to him.

When God saw how dearly Abraham loved his son, and how obedient and loving Isaac was toward his father, he thought, "I must prove Abraham this once more, and see whether he loves me better than he loves the child I have given." So he called to Abraham one day, and Abraham answered, "Behold, here am I." Then God said, "Take your son, your only son, Isaac, whom you love so much, and go into the land of Moriah. There give him back to me as an offering upon an altar, which you must build at the place I will show."

Abraham did not know the reason why God should ask him to give Isaac back as an offering. He could not understand how the promises concerning Isaac would be fulfilled if now he must offer Isaac upon an altar, just like the lambs that he had given to God at other times. But Abraham believed that God understood why, and so he was not afraid to obey.

The land of Moriah was some distance from Abraham's tent, and the journey there would require a few days' time. Abraham knew this, and he prepared to start at once. He called two young men servants and Isaac, then saddled his donkey, and they started away. They took wood and fire with which to burn the offering, and traveled on and on for two days, sleeping at night under the trees. On the third day Abraham saw the mountain where God wanted him to build the altar and offer his gift. He left the servants with the donkey to wait by the roadside, while he and Isaac should go on alone. Isaac carried the wood upon his shoulder, and Abraham took the vessel containing the fire.

As they climbed the mountainside together, Isaac began to wonder why his father had forgotten to bring a lamb for an offering. He did not know what God had asked Abraham to give. He did not understand why they were going so far from home to build the altar. So he said, "My father, see, here is wood and fire for the altar, but where is the lamb for an offering?" Abraham replied, "God will provide himself a lamb."

When they reached the place God had appointed, Abraham built an altar, laid the wood upon it, and then bound Isaac's hands and feet and placed him upon the wood. Next he took his knife, and was about to kill Isaac when a loud voice called to him out of the sky, "Abraham! Abraham!" The old man stopped to listen, and the angel of God said to him, "Do not harm Isaac. Now I know that you love God even better than you love your child. Untie his hands and his feet, and let him go." At this Abraham saw a ram caught by its horns in a thicket nearby. He took this animal and offered it as a gift to God instead of offering his son Isaac.

Afterward the angel called to Abraham from the sky again, and said, "Because you have not withheld your dearly loved child from me, I will surely bless you and will cause your descendants to be as many as the stars in the heavens and as the sands upon the seashore. And I will bless all the nations of the earth through your descendants, because you have obeyed my voice."

No doubt it was a happy father and son who walked down the mountainside together; for now Abraham knew that he had surely pleased God, and Isaac knew that his life was precious in God's sight. Abraham called the name of the place where he built the altar, Jehovah-jireh, which means in his language, "The Lord will provide." Then they returned to the young men servants who were waiting by the roadside, and then journeyed on to their home at Beersheba, where Abraham had planted trees and dug a well some time before this story. Here Abraham lived for many years.

Gen. 23:1–25:18

When Sarah, Isaac's mother, was one hundred and twenty-seven years old, she died. Abraham had no place to bury her, so he bought a field from a Hittite who was named Ephron. The field contained a cave such as the people of Canaan used for burial places, and Abraham buried Sarah in this cave. The field and the cave were called by the name of Machpelah.

After Sarah's death, Abraham and Isaac felt lonely. Isaac was now grown to manhood, and Abraham thought he was old enough to be married. The parents usually chose wives for their sons, and husbands for their daughters, in those times, and Abraham wished to choose a good wife for Isaac. He knew that the women who lived in Canaan were idol-worshipers, and that they would not teach their children to love and to worship the true God. Because he wanted Isaac's children to serve God, he would not choose a young woman of Canaan to be Isaac's wife.

Then Abraham remembered the news that had come to

him from his brother Nahor, who lived at Haran, the place in the country of Mesopotamia where he had stopped on his journey to Canaan, and where his aged father had died. Nahor, he had been told, was now the father of twelve sons, some of whom had married and become fathers also. "Perhaps I can go back to my own people at Haran," thought Abraham, "and find among them a wife for Isaac." So he called his trusted servant, Eliezer, told him about his desire, and asked him to journey back to Haran and try to find a God-fearing wife for Isaac.

Eliezer knew that such a journey would require many days' time and would be attended by many dangers along the way. He knew, too, that Abraham's people might not be willing to send a daughter so far from home to become the wife of a man whom they had never met. But because he was a faithful servant and loved his master, Abraham, Eliezer said, "I will go."

Then the long journey began. Eliezer took with him ten camels, several attendant servants, and many valuable presents. For days and days they traveled, crossing valleys, hills, and rivers, and edging alongside the great, lonely desert. By and by they came to the land of Mesopotamia, to the northern part, called Padan-aram, and then at last their tired camels stopped outside the city of Haran and knelt down near a well.

It was evening time, and the women of the city were coming to this well to fill their pitchers with water. Eliezer had learned to trust in Abraham's God, and now he lifted up his heart and prayed that God would send out to this well the young woman who would be suitable for Isaac's wife. "Let it come to pass, O Lord," he prayed, "that the young woman of whom I shall ask a drink may offer to draw water for my camels also. By this sign I shall know that she is the one whom you have chosen, for Abraham's sake, to be the wife of Isaac."

While Eliezer was praying, a beautiful young woman approached, with an earthen pitcher upon her shoulder. Eliezer waited until she had filled the pitcher with water, then he asked for a drink. Although he was a stranger, she spoke kindly to him and said she would draw water for his camels also. Again and again she filled her pitcher and poured its contents into the trough that the thirsty animals might drink. When she had done this, Eliezer gave her some of the beautiful presents that he had brought, and asked whose daughter she was and whether her people could supply lodging for him and for his camels. At her reply that she was the granddaughter of Nahor, Abraham's brother, Eliezer knew that his prayer had been answered, and he bowed his head and worshiped God. Then Rebekah—for this was the young woman's name—told Eliezer that there was plenty of room in her father's house to lodge them all, and she hurried to tell what had happened at the well and to show the beautiful presents that Eliezer had given her.

When her brother Laban heard her story and saw the costly ornaments that Eliezer had given to Rebekah, he ran eagerly to meet the strangers at the well and to invite them to come in. "We have room for you and for your camels," he told them, and they went with him into the city. Laban now showed the same kindness to his guests that Abraham and Lot had shown to their angel visitors. He first brought water to wash their feet and then set food before them.

But Eliezer could not eat. "First let me tell why I have come," he said. "I am Abraham's servant, and God has blessed my master greatly, giving him flocks and herds, silver and gold, and many servants, besides camels and donkeys. God also gave to him and Sarah a son in their old age, and now Abraham has given all his great riches to his son. But as yet this son, Isaac, has no wife, and Abraham will not take a wife for him from the daughters of Canaan, because they worship idols. He has sent me, therefore, to you, his kinsfolk, to find a wife for Isaac." Eliezer told also how Rebekah had come to the well and how in answer to his prayer she had offered drink to him and to his thirsty animals.

Rebekah's father and brother Laban were willing to let her go back with Eliezer because they believed that God had sent him. And Rebekah, too, was willing to go. Eliezer was grateful to know of their willingness, and he bowed his head once more to worship the great God who had helped him on his journey. Afterward he enjoyed the feast that Rebekah's people had prepared for them. That same night he gave other presents of silver and gold and beautiful clothing to Rebekah, and to her mother and brother.

The next morning Eliezer said, "Now let me return to my master." Laban and his mother did not want to let Rebekah leave them so soon. "Can you not stay for a few more days?" they asked. But when Eliezer insisted that he must go at once, they called Rebekah, and she said, "I will go." So they bade her good-bye and sent her away with her nurse and other attending maids.

On the homeward journey Rebekah and her maids rode the camels, and Eliezer led the way to Canaan. Very likely they traveled the same road that Abraham had traveled many years before, when he went with Sarah and Lot to the land that God had promised. At last they drew near to the place where Abraham and Isaac now lived. The evening shadows were stealing through the trees, and Isaac was out in the fields alone, thinking about God, when he saw the camels coming. He hurried to meet them, and Rebekah, seeing him, asked who he was. "This is my master, Isaac," Eliezer replied, and Rebekah alighted from her camel and covered her face with a veil.

When Isaac met them, Eliezer told how God had answered his prayers and had sent Rebekah to him. Isaac took her to his mother's tent, and she became his wife. He loved her, and did not grieve any more because of his mother's death.

The time passed on, and finally Abraham died, too. He had reached the age of one hundred and seventy-five. Ishmael heard of his death and came to help Isaac bury his father. They placed his body in the cave where Sarah had been buried. After that time Isaac became the possessor of all his father's wealth.

THE STORY OF JACOB AND JOSEPH

Gen. 25:19–27:41

After some years, a change took place in Isaac's home life. Two children now played about his tent door— two little boys. They were his sons. One of them, the older, was named Esau. His hair was red and it grew all over his body. Although he was a queer-looking child, Esau was loved dearly by his father, Isaac. The younger boy was named Jacob. He was not at all like his brother, and it may have been because of his thoughtful actions that he was loved the better by his mother, Rebekah.

When Esau and Jacob grew older, their playtime hours grew less and they were taught to work. They learned to take care of their father's cattle and sheep. Esau was fond of hunting, and would often take his bow and arrow and go out to the woods in search of deer. Not only did he know how to kill the deer, but he knew also how to dress and cook the meat that he brought home from his hunting trips. This pleased Isaac very much, and because he liked to eat the venison that Esau prepared he loved Esau better than he loved Jacob.

There is a custom among the people of those lands to give the eldest son twice as much of the property upon the death of the father as the other children receive. This is called the "birthright." And Esau, being Isaac's eldest son, was entitled to the birthright.

But the boy Esau cared little about his birthright. He even despised it. His younger brother, Jacob, thought much about the birthright and wished that it might be given to him instead of to Esau. He knew that he should be glad to receive his father's blessing and the double portion of all his wealth, and even the tents in which they lived, and the servants who belonged to his father's household.

One day when Esau came home from his work in the field he saw that Jacob had just prepared a dish of tempting food. And he was very hungry, so he asked Jacob to give him at once some of the food to eat. Jacob answered, "I will give it all to you if you will sell me your birthright today." Esau grew hungrier than ever when he smelled the good food in Jacob's dish, and he cared more for his appetite than he did for his birthright. "What can this birthright profit me, anyhow," he questioned, "seeing that I am certain to die anyway?" So he sold his birthright for something to eat. Now, it was very wrong for Esau to despise the good things that Isaac had planned to give to him. And after it was too late to buy back the lost birthright, Esau became very sorry for what he had done.

The years passed by, and Isaac moved into another part of the country. Here he planted fields of grain, and God caused them to yield an abundant harvest. God also blessed him more by increasing his riches until he became so great that his neighbors envied him. They thought he was a mighty prince among them, and they did not care to have him live in their country because he was so much greater than they. Isaac chose to go away rather than to have trouble with his neighbors, so he gathered together all his wealth and all his servants, and moved once more to another part of Canaan. Here he built an altar and worshiped God. Afterward his servants dug a well and found good water. Then Isaac called the name of the place Beersheba.

Isaac lived at Beersheba for a long time, and finally his eyes grew dim with age. No longer could he look out upon the good things that God had given him, and he thought that soon he must die. He wished to give the birthright and his blessing to Esau. Perhaps he did not remember that God had promised the birthright to Jacob, or he may have forgotten about the incident because he was now old and feeble. He called Esau, and said, "My son, take your bow and arrow and go into the woods and hunt one more deer and bring to me the delicious food that you can prepare. After I have eaten of it I shall give you my blessing, for I am soon to die."

Esau hurried away at his father's bidding. He was older now and wished that he had not sold his birthright. But he had done other things that were not right, for he had married two wives who were Canaanitish women, and this had grieved Isaac and Rebekah very much.

Rebekah did not think that Esau was worthy to receive

his father's blessing. She wanted her younger son, Jacob, to become heir to God's promises, and when she heard Isaac's instructions to Esau she thought of a plan by which she might secure the promised blessing for Jacob. "My husband cannot see," she reasoned, "and I will send Jacob to him instead of Esau. I will cook the tender meat of two young kids, and season the food just as Esau prepares it. Then I will clothe Jacob in Esau's raiment and thus cause my blind husband to think that Esau has come."

At first Jacob feared to try to deceive his dear old father lest his deception be found out and he should receive a curse instead of a blessing. But Rebekah urged him to obey her orders. "Let the sin be upon my own head," she declared, "for you must receive your father's blessing." And Jacob obeyed. But, although he secured the blessing, we shall see later how the sin of his deception fell upon his own head, because sin always acts upon the evil-doer himself and brings trouble and sorrow.

Isaac was surprised when Jacob approached with the dish of food that Rebekah had prepared. He knew that Esau had not been absent long enough to hunt and kill a deer and then prepare the meat so soon. "How is it that you have come so soon?" he asked, and Jacob replied, "Your God helped me to find the deer at once." Still Isaac wondered how it could be that Esau had returned so much sooner than usual, and because the voice sounded like Jacob's he said, "Come near to me, that I may know whether you are indeed my very son Esau." Now Rebekah had fastened the skin of a hairy animal upon Jacob's hands and neck lest Isaac feel of them and discover the deception, and when the blind old man touched the hairy hands he said, "These are Esau's hands." Finally he ate of the delicious meat and then blessed Jacob with the blessing of his grandfather Abraham.

Esau came with his dish after Jacob had gone away. "Rise up, my father, and eat of my venison," he said, "then give me your blessing." "Who are you?" exclaimed Isaac in dismay; and when Esau replied, "I am your very son Esau," the old man trembled with fear. "Some one has come in your stead," he told Esau, "and to him I have given the blessing."

Esau knew at once that Jacob had secured the blessing that was his. "Alas!" cried the poor man, "my brother has taken away both my birthright and my blessing." And Esau wept bitterly. "Have you not one blessing for me also?" he entreated. Isaac was deeply troubled. "How can I bless you, seeing that I have given the best of everything to your brother?" Still Esau pleaded for a blessing, and finally Isaac blessed him too, with a lesser promise of greatness.

After this time Esau's heart was filled with hatred toward his brother. "Soon our father will die," he thought, "and then I shall kill Jacob and take all the possessions and all the power that has been given to him." And with these wicked thoughts he consoled himself in his disappointment and grief.

When Rebekah heard of Esau's intention to kill his brother Jacob as soon as their father, Isaac, should die, she sent for Jacob at once. "You must prepare to go far away," she told him, "because Esau is angry and plans to kill you when your father dies. Let me send you to my brother, Laban, who lives at Haran. Remain there with him for a while, and possibly Esau will forget his anger and wicked plans. Then you can come back again to me; for why should I lose both you and your father?"

Rebekah did not tell Isaac about Esau's anger and about her fears for Jacob's safety. But now that she wanted to send Jacob back to her girlhood home in order to escape from Esau's anger she planned another reason for wishing to send him away. She came to her blind husband and said, "I am very unhappy because our son Esau has taken heathen women to become his wives. If Jacob should marry a daughter of our heathen neighbors, I should wish to die. Send him back to my brother's house, that he may take a wife from among my own people."

Isaac also had been grieved when Esau married women who were idol-worshipers. Now he thought, "God's promise, which was first given to my father Abraham, then to me, will be given next to my son Jacob and to his children. If he should marry a heathen woman, then his children would not be taught to worship the true God. He must not marry a heathen woman!" So he called Jacob, and said, "Do not take a wife of the daughters of Canaan, but go back to

Padanaram and take there a wife from your mother's relatives. And God's blessing shall be upon you, and he shall give
you the blessings of your grandfather Abraham."

Jacob then bade his mother and his blind old father
good-bye, and started out on his long journey. He took no
camel to ride upon and no servant for a companion, but
journeyed all alone. He feared his brother's wrath, and did
not know whether he ever could return again to his home
and feel safe. His birthright now could do him no good
because the double portion of his father's wealth would not
become his own until after his father's death, and if he
should remain until that time he believed that his brother
would surely kill him. Poor, discouraged Jacob! He must
have felt unhappy indeed as he climbed the rocky hillslopes
of Canaan and hurried away from the only home he had ever
known. We do not know what his thoughts were as he traveled alone all the day, but perhaps he thought that Esau
might try to overtake him and kill him before he should get
far away. Perhaps he felt sorry because he had deceived his
dear, old father, whom he might never see again. Perhaps he
repented because he had bought Esau's birthright. Whatever
may have been his thoughts as he walked along the dusty
road, some One was listening to each and all of them. That
One was God.

By and by the sun went down, and Jacob may have felt
lonelier than ever with only the dark sky above him. But as
he was now very tired, he chose a stone for his pillow, and,
wrapping his cloak about him, lay down on the ground to
sleep. While he slept he saw in a dream a wonderful ladder
the top of which reached to heaven. He saw beautiful angels

climbing up and down upon the ladder. And standing at the top he saw God. He dreamed that God spoke to him and said, "I am the God of your grandfather Abraham, and the God of your father Isaac. The land upon which you are lying I will give to you and to your descendants. And your descendants shall be many, as many as the particles of dust upon the earth. Through your family I will bless all the people of the earth. Now, I am with you, and will be with you wherever you go, and will protect you and bring you again to this land. I will never leave you until I have fulfilled this promise."

Jacob awoke from his dream and looked about. Although he saw no one, he felt sure that he was not alone, because the God of his father had promised to be with him. He arose early in the morning and took the stone that he had used for a pillow and set it upright. Then he poured some oil upon it, to consecrate it to God. He called the name of the place Bethel, which means, "The house of God." Then he made a vow and promised to give back to God a tenth of all that God should give him if indeed God would go with him and bless him as he had promised.

After this wonderful dream Jacob's heart must have felt lighter as he hurried on his way. And every day he drew nearer the end of his long, tiresome journey. Then one evening, after he had left the lonely desert far behind, he saw some men, in a field, near a well. Round about them three flocks of sheep were lying down and waiting to be watered. This sight may have reminded him of his father's flocks at home, which he had often cared for. He came nearer and spoke to the men. "Where are you from?" he asked; and when they replied that they were men of Haran he knew that at last he was near his uncle Laban's home. "Do you know a man of Haran named Laban?" he asked eagerly, and they answered, "Yes, we know him; and, see, here comes his daughter Rachel with his sheep." Jacob saw a beautiful young shepherdess approaching and he hurried to meet her. He rolled the stone away from the well and watered her sheep, then told her that he was her cousin, the son of her father's sister, Rebekah. His joy upon seeing one of his relatives after such a long, lonely journey brought tears to Jacob's eyes and he wept as he kissed the beautiful girl.

No doubt Laban had told Rachel about the strange men who had come from his granduncle Abraham a long time ago and who had taken his sister to become the wife of Abraham's son, Isaac. And so Rachel hurried home to tell her father that his sister's son had arrived from Canaan and was now taking charge of his flock of sheep at the well.

Gen. 29:13–31:55

When Rachel told her father, Laban, that Jacob had arrived, he hurried out to meet his nephew and to welcome him to his home. He was glad to hear tidings from his sister, Rebekah, and to speak face-to-face with her favorite son. At first he showed much kindness to Jacob.

As the days passed by Jacob willingly assisted his uncle at his work. Then at the end of the first month Laban said, "Let me pay you for your services. What do you ask for wages?" Jacob replied, "I will serve you faithfully for seven years if at the end of that time you will give me your beautiful daughter, Rachel, to be my wife." This may seem a strange request, but Jacob loved Rachel and wished to marry her. He loved her so much that to him the seven years of hard toil seemed only a few days.

At the end of the period of service Jacob reminded his uncle that the time for his marriage had arrived. Laban then arranged a marriage feast. He invited many friends to attend the wedding. In the evening he brought the bride to Jacob. A large veil was thrown about her that no one might look upon her face. This was the usual custom of those people, and even Jacob could not see the face of the woman he was taking to become his wife.

After the ceremony had ended and Jacob was permitted to see his wife's face he saw—not the beautiful Rachel, whom he loved so dearly and for whom he had toiled seven years, but her elder sister, Leah. Now Leah did not look beautiful to Jacob, and he had not loved her. He had not wanted to marry her. How unhappy he felt when he realized that his uncle had deceived him! Perhaps he remembered how he had deceived his blind father, and how he had cheated his brother out of the blessing. Now he was suffering from the same kind of sins that he himself had committed against others. And now he understood how painful it is to be deceived or cheated.

When Jacob demanded an explanation of the deception, Laban said that it was not customary in their country to allow the younger daughter to marry first. "If you will serve me for seven years longer, you may have Rachel also for your wife," Laban added; and because Jacob loved Rachel he decided to remain with his uncle for seven more years.

When the fourteen years had passed by, Jacob desired to return again to Canaan. But Laban was unwilling to let him go. "While you have been with me," he told Jacob, "the Lord has blessed me for your sake." When Jacob insisted that he needed to provide for his own family, Laban agreed to let him have a part of the cattle and sheep and goats. These Jacob separated from Laban's flocks and herds and placed in charge of his sons. He continued to have charge of Laban's flocks, but kept his own at a distance of three days' journey from Laban's home. And God blessed Jacob and increased his possessions until soon he became rich. He bought camels and donkeys, and owned many servants. And God gave him eleven sons and one daughter.

When Jacob's riches increased, Laban's sons became envious of him. They said that he had gotten his riches dishonestly. Laban, too, began to feel unkindly toward him. Then the angel of God spoke to Jacob in a dream and comforted him. "I am the God of Bethel," the angel said, "where you anointed the stone, and where you made a vow to me. The time has come for you to return again to your people in Canaan. I will be with you."

Jacob remembered that Laban had been unwilling before to let him go when he expressed a desire to return to his father. Now he feared that Laban would not allow him to take his daughters, Leah and Rachel, to far-off Canaan, so he decided to go away secretly. He waited until Laban went to shear his sheep. Then he called Leah and Rachel out into the field and told them that their father no longer felt kindly toward him. He told them also that God had talked to him and had charged him to return again to Canaan. And they replied, "We are ready to go with you, for our father has sold us." They believed that God was with Jacob.

Busy days followed, in which Jacob prepared to start out on the long road over which he had traveled twenty years before. The sheep and the goats and the cattle and the camels and the donkeys were all collected from the fields where they had been grazing on the tender grass. The servants drove the animals, while Jacob's wives and children rode on camels. Across the fields they went, and onto the road that wound along the lonely wilderness, where wild mountains rose on the one side and dreary desert sand stretched far away on the other side. Finally they came to a camping place in mount Gilead where they stopped to rest.

But we must not forget that things were happening back at Haran. Someone told Laban that Jacob had gone away and had taken all his possessions. Laban was angry because Jacob had departed, and still more vexed with him because he had stolen away in secret. "I shall overtake him," thought the angry man; and possibly he planned to compel Jacob to return again to Haran. He took with him several men and hurried in pursuit of Jacob's company. For seven days they followed fast, and at last they saw the tents that Jacob had pitched in mount Gilead. But before they reached the place, God spoke to Laban and warned him not to harm Jacob.

This warning from God caused Laban to feel less angry toward Jacob, and soon their quarrel was ended. Afterward Jacob set up a stone for a pillar and the other men gathered stones together in a heap. Laban called this heap of stones Mizpah, which means, "A watchtower." And he said to Jacob, "May God watch over us while we are absent from each other." Then, bidding his daughters and their children an affectionate farewell, he turned back toward his home at Haran, leaving Jacob and his family to continue their journey toward Canaan.

Gen. 32–35

Although twenty years had passed since Jacob's flight from Canaan, he had never forgotten the fear that had driven him to Haran. And the memory of that fear still troubled him—what if Esau should never forgive him?

God knew about Jacob's fear, and he sent a company of angels to meet him. After this Jacob felt more courageous and sent some messengers to his brother to announce his coming. He felt that unless Esau should welcome him home he could not be happy in Canaan.

But Esau no longer lived in Canaan. He had moved with

his family to the country of Edom, which lies south and east of the Dead Sea. There the messengers found him and told him that Jacob was returning to Canaan. He sent word back with the messengers that he would come to meet Jacob. Four hundred men were coming with him.

This news from Esau troubled Jacob greatly. He thought that Esau was intending to kill him and his wives and children. He quickly divided his company into two bands and sent one before the other. But first he sent a valuable present of sheep and oxen, camels, and donkeys to his brother, hoping thereby to arouse a kindly feeling in Esau's heart. After nightfall he moved his camp across the brook, and then returned alone. Then in the darkness a strange man took hold of him and wrestled all the night. Jacob wrestled earnestly, and neither of them gained advantage of the other. When the morning began to dawn Jacob saw that he had been wrestling with the angel of God. The angel said, "Let me go, for the day is breaking." But Jacob answered, "I will not let you go until you bless me." Then the angel asked, "What is your name?" and he said, "My name is Jacob." The angel told him that his name should thereafter be Israel, because he had wrestled with God. Israel means, "A prince of God." When the angel departed, Jacob was crippled in his thigh, for the angel had struck it. Jacob called the name of the place Peniel, which means, "The face of God," because there he saw God face-to-face and received the blessing that he sought.

When the sun arose, Jacob crossed the brook and joined the company of his family again. And soon he saw his brother Esau coming to meet him. No doubt his heart beat fast as he arranged his wives and children in separate groups and then hurried forward to be the first to greet Esau. According to custom, he bowed himself to the ground in a very humble manner as he approached his brother. Seven times he bowed thus. Then Esau rushed forward and embraced Jacob very affectionately and kissed him. The two brothers wept for joy, and all the bitterness of the past seemed to be forgotten.

Afterward Jacob presented his wives and their children to his brother, and told him how God had blessed him while he lived at Haran.

Esau inquired about the animals that he had met, and Jacob told him that they were his present. Esau at first refused to accept them because he, too, had much wealth; but finally he consented to take them as a gift from his brother.

After their short visit together, Esau returned again to his home in the land of Edom, and Jacob journeyed on to Canaan. At Shechem he bought a field, where he built an altar and worshiped God. He felt very grateful because God had given him a safe journey from Haran. Later he moved to Bethel, at God's command, and built another altar in memory of the promise that God had given to him when he slept at that place while fleeing from his brother. God appeared to him again, and once more told him that he should be called Jacob no longer, but Israel. God also enlarged the promise that he had made concerning Jacob's descendants, and told him that kings should be born among them in the coming years.

From Bethel, Jacob and his family moved southward

toward his old home at Hebron, where his father, Isaac, still lived. Many years had passed since he had traveled that same road, alone and afraid; now he was returning to his father's house bringing with him enough servants to form two companies, besides his own family. Surely God had blessed him; and his heart was glad.

But before they arrived at Hebron a sad thing happened. Rachel died, leaving a tiny baby boy, whom she had named Benjamin. Jacob buried her at Bethlehem, and set a pillar upon her grave. Afterward he came to Hebron.

Isaac was now a very old man, and for many years he had been expecting to die. No doubt he rejoiced when Jacob returned safely from his long sojourn at Haran, bringing with him twelve sons and a daughter. But Isaac did not live much longer after this time, and when he died—at the age of one hundred and eighty years—Esau came and helped Jacob bury him.

Among Jacob's twelve sons was one whom he loved better than the others. That one was Joseph—the eleventh son born in his household and the eldest son of Rachel, his beloved wife. Joseph was a good boy indeed, just the kind of boy that a father can trust to do right. Sad to say, his elder brothers were not so careful always to do right, and their wrong-doing brought much pain to Jacob's heart.

Because Jacob loved Joseph so tenderly, his brothers became envious of him. And when Jacob made a wonderful coat of many colors and gave it to Joseph, the older sons allowed a bitter feeling of hatred to creep into their wicked hearts. One day while Joseph was in the field with four of them he saw their evil conduct, and on his return home he told his father how wrongly they had behaved. By doing this he increased the bitter feeling that was growing against him in his brothers' hearts, for wicked people are always angered when someone exposes their wickedness. Joseph's brothers would no longer speak kindly to him.

Joseph was now about seventeen years old. One night he had a strange dream. He told his brothers about it. "We were together in the field binding sheaves," he said, "and my sheaf stood upright while yours bowed down around it."

"Do you think you are some day going to rule over us?" the brothers asked in angry voices; and they hated him even more than before.

Soon Joseph dreamed again, a dream more strange than the other one had been. This time he saw the sun, the moon, and eleven stars bowing down before him. If such a dream had any meaning at all, how could it mean anything else than that he should some day become a ruler before whom his relatives should bow themselves? Joseph wondered about the dream and he told it to his father and brothers. His father was displeased, because he thought it would be wrong for a man to bow down before his son. That would seem to make Joseph greater, better, and wiser than he. Still he wondered what such a dream could mean, and he thought much about the matter.

Now Jacob and his family were living at Hebron, where Abraham had lived so long ago with his many servants and flocks and herds. Jacob's flocks were so large that they could not find enough pasture nearby at all seasons, and sometimes they had to be taken far from home to find grass and water. The time came again when it was necessary to find pasture elsewhere, so Jacob sent his ten eldest sons to Shechem with the cattle and sheep. After they had been away from home for some weeks, Jacob sent Joseph on an errand to learn whether or not the young men were getting on well with their work.

Joseph started out alone on his long journey of fifty miles to Shechem. When he came to the place, he could not find his brothers, nor their flocks. He did not know where to go in search of them. Soon a man who lived in a town nearby met him and told him that his brothers had gone to Dothan, to find better pasture. Joseph then journeyed on, over the hills and across the valleys, to Dothan, which was fifteen miles farther from Hebron, and there he saw the flocks feeding on the green grass long before he arrived at the place.

When the brothers saw a young man coming across the fields clad in a beautifully colored coat they said at once to each other, "Here comes the Dreamer. Let us kill him, and we shall see what will become of his dreams." The eldest brother, Reuben, felt more kindly toward Joseph and wished to save his life. But he feared the others would not listen if he should tell them not to harm Joseph, so he said, "Let us not kill him; only throw him down into this pit and leave him alone to die." The others quickly agreed to do as Reuben said, and when Joseph approached they seized him, tore off his beautiful coat, and roughly put him into the deep pit. Then they sat down on the ground and ate their lunch, paying no heed to his pitiful cries.

Now Reuben did not intend to leave Joseph alone to die. He planned to come back as soon as the others should go away, and rescue his young brother from such a sad death. But it was not going to be Reuben, after all, who should draw Joseph from the pit.

While the brothers were eating their lunch, Reuben went to another part of the field, and during his absence a company of traveling merchants came riding by on camels. Some of these travelers were called Ishmaelites, because they were descendants of Ishmael, and they were going to Egypt to sell rich spices and perfumed gum, which had been gathered from trees in other countries. "Now," thought Judah, another of Joseph's elder brothers, "here is an opportunity to make some money, and to get rid of our brother without letting him die." So, calling his brothers, he said, "It would be better to sell Joseph to these merchants than to leave him to die in the pit; for even though we despise him, he is our brother." The others were quite willing to sell Joseph; so they drew him out of the pit, and soon he saw himself being exchanged to the Ishmaelites for twenty pieces of silver.

Poor Joseph! this was a sad time for him. Now he knew that he should be taken far away by rough strangers who had become his masters. Now he was sold! All his pleading and all his tears did not soften the hearts of his wicked brothers, who greedily divided the money among themselves and supposed that they were forever rid of him. Perhaps they did not even watch the caravan as it moved slowly away toward the south, and disappeared from view behind the green-clad hills.

After the Ishmaelites passed on and the brothers too went away to different parts of the field, Reuben came hurrying back to the pit. Stooping down, he called to Joseph; but no answer came from the dark hole. Again and again he called, thinking perhaps that Joseph had fallen asleep, but still the silence was unbroken—Joseph did not reply. Then, after a while, Reuben knew that his brother was not there. What should he do? Now he forgot he had been afraid to let his brothers know that he had intended all the while to rescue Joseph from their hands. He forgot everything except the fact that Joseph had disappeared. He believed some dreadful thing had happened to the poor boy. Perhaps a wild beast had devoured him. Tearing his clothes as people did when they were in deep trouble, he returned to his brothers and said, "The child is gone, and what shall I do?" Being the eldest son, he felt that he should have taken care of his brother.

Next came the question of how they should account to

their father for the disappearance of his favorite son. Finally they decided to dip Joseph's coat in blood, killing a young kid for this purpose, and take the blood-stained garment back to their father, telling him that they had found it in that condition. We see that they were planning to use a wicked lie to cover up their wicked deed.

Jacob was alarmed when his sons returned without Joseph. When he saw the blood-dyed coat he knew it was the very one that he had made for the lost boy, and he believed at once that wild animals had torn Joseph in pieces. Tearing his own garments apart and dressing himself in rough cloth called sackcloth, he sat down and mourned bitterly for many days, refusing to be comforted.

Gen. 37:36–40:23

At the end of their long, dusty journey the Ishmaelites arrived with Joseph in Egypt. Here Joseph found himself surrounded by a people who spoke a different language from his own. And here he saw large cities, wonderful temples for idol-worship, mighty pyramids, and the great River Nile. How strange all these things must have seemed to this boy, who had always lived in tents!

The Ishmaelites took Joseph to the city where the king of Egypt lived, and there they sold him to an officer in the king's army. Joseph could never forget how terror-stricken he had felt when his own brothers sold him as a slave. But he was a sensible young man, and when he realized that he was indeed a slave he tried to be obedient to his master. And

God did not forget him, nor the wonderful dreams he had given to Joseph when he was yet at home. God was now preparing Joseph for the time when those dreams should come true. Although Joseph could not understand God's plan, he trusted in God to help him do right.

The Egyptian officer who bought Joseph was named Potiphar. He was a very rich man and had many other servants. Joseph soon learned the speech of the Egyptians, and because he showed a cheerful, obedient spirit, Potiphar took special notice of him. He saw that Joseph was always honest and that he had a good understanding of business affairs. After a while he gave all the oversight of his household and his riches into Joseph's care, and for Joseph's sake God blessed the Egyptian officer with greater riches. For several years Joseph remained in Potiphar's house—a slave in name only, for in reality he was the ruler over his fellow slaves and the caretaker of his master's wealth.

Then there came a sudden change. Potiphar's wife was not a good woman, and she often tried to persuade Joseph to do wickedly. Because he would not, she finally became angry with him and accused him falsely to her husband. Potiphar believed the lie that she told, and to punish Joseph he thrust the noble young man into the king's prison. How cruel this was! Perhaps Joseph wondered why he must suffer so often because of the sins of other people. To be a slave had seemed bad enough; to be thrust into prison while trying to do right was even worse. No doubt Joseph suffered much because of this unjust act.

But Joseph was not the kind of person to fret and pout because of trouble. He showed a cheerful spirit even in the prison, and his manly face soon attracted the attention of the prison-keeper. Day after day the keeper watched him, and finally he decided that Joseph was the very one he needed to help care for the other prisoners. After a while he gave Joseph full charge of all the prisoners, and doubtless Joseph was once more as busy as he had been in Potiphar's house.

About that time Pharaoh, the king of Egypt, became much displeased with two of his special servants—the chief butler, who served him with wines, and the chief baker, who served him with bread. Because of his displeasure he put both of them into prison, and Joseph cared for them there.

One morning Joseph found these men looking unusually sad. "Why are you so troubled?" he asked. And they replied, "We have had strange dreams, and there is no one here to tell us the meaning of them. In the king's court there are wise men who often tell the meaning of dreams, but we can not send for them to come to us in prison."

"Surely God knows the meaning of your dreams," Joseph told them, "and I am his servant. Tell me, therefore, what you have dreamed. He may reveal to me the true meaning."

The chief butler was first to tell his dream. "I saw a grapevine with three branches," he said, "and while I looked upon it the buds shot forth and became blossoms, and the blossoms became clusters of grapes. Then I squeezed the juice of the grapes into Pharaoh's cup, which I held in my hand. This I gave to the king as I used to do when I stood by his table."

God made Joseph know the meaning of the dream, and Joseph said, "The three branches that you saw are three days; after that time you will be restored to your former position in the king's palace. But I beg you to remember me when it shall be well with you again, and make mention of me to Pharaoh; for I have been stolen from my father's house and sold a captive among these people. And for no wrong-doing of mine I have been thrust into this prison."

The chief baker now told what his dream had been, and wished Joseph to tell its meaning. "There were three baskets upon my head," he said, "and in the topmost one there were bakemeats for the king's table. While I held them, the birds flew down and ate the contents of the topmost basket."

Through the wisdom of God, Joseph knew the meaning of this dream, too. He felt sorry to tell its meaning, though, because he knew that his words would bring more grief to the chief baker's heart. But the chief baker expected him to tell, so he said, "In your dream the three baskets mean three days. At that time the king will take you from the prison and hang your body upon a tree, and the birds will eat your flesh."

Three days later Pharaoh held a great feast for his servants in honor of his birthday. During the feast he removed both the chief butler and the chief baker from the prison and disposed of them just as Joseph had said he would. But the chief butler soon forgot about Joseph, and two years passed by before he remembered to speak to the king about the one who had been kind to him while he was in prison.

Gen. 41

One morning Pharaoh wakened from sleep wondering about the meaning of two strange dreams that he had dreamed during the night. He called the wise men of Egypt to tell him what the dreams meant, but they could not. Then he felt greatly troubled.

When the chief butler heard about the king's distress, he thought at once of his own experiences when he was in prison. And he remembered Joseph's kindness. How long he had forgotten that noble young man! Now he told Pharaoh about Joseph, and immediately the king sent for him.

Joseph was busy caring for the prisoners and thinking perhaps that the chief butler had forever forgotten him when the messenger came from the king's palace. "Pharaoh wishes to see you: Come at once," the messenger said.

Joseph shaved his face and changed his prison clothes for clean, fresh garments. Then he hurried to the royal palace, wondering as he went why Pharaoh had sent for him. "If only he would grant me liberty," he thought, "how happy I should be!"

At the palace Pharaoh was anxiously waiting to see him. Others, too, were waiting, and all were feeling deeply troubled. "If this strange young man cannot help, what shall we do?" they were wondering. Then there came a sound of footsteps outside the door, and Joseph was brought into their midst. Then Pharaoh spoke:

"I have heard of you," he said, "that you can tell the true meaning of dreams. And I have dreamed two dreams that trouble me greatly; therefore I have sent for you because none of the wise men of Egypt can tell me what these dreams mean."

Joseph replied, "This wisdom does not belong to me, but to the God whom I serve. Tell me what your dreams were, and he will give the meaning of them."

And Pharaoh answered: "In my dream I was standing by the River Nile, and presently I saw seven fat cattle come up out of the river and feed in the green meadow. Later I saw seven other cattle come up out of the river and stand upon the bank. These seven were very lean, and I saw them approach the seven fat cattle and eat them up. Still they were as thin as they had been at the first. Then I awoke.

"Afterward I fell asleep and dreamed again, and saw seven ears of corn grow up out of a stalk. Full, good ears they were, and while I was looking at them seven other ears sprang up after them—withered, thin, and blasted with the east wind. These thin ears devoured the good ones, and once more I awoke."

"Your dreams are indeed wonderful," Joseph told the king, "and both of them have the same meaning. By them God is making known to you what he is about to do.

"The seven fat cattle are seven years, and so also are the seven good, full ears of corn. And in like manner the seven lean cattle and the seven thin, withered ears are seven years that shall follow the first seven. God is making known to you by these dreams that there shall be seven years of plenty throughout all the land of Egypt, and afterward there shall be seven years of famine. These years of famine shall be so severe that the seven years of plenty shall be forgotten, and everything shall be eaten up throughout the land.

"God has given you these two dreams to show you that these things will surely come to pass soon. He has warned you in this manner to prepare for the time of famine, lest it come upon you and destroy every living creature in your kingdom. It will be well for you to appoint a wise man to look after the food supply. Let him, during the seven plentiful years, lay aside enough each year to make sure of enough for all your people during the years when nothing shall grow."

Pharaoh and the attendants who stood near his throne listened attentively to Joseph's words, and when he had finished speaking the king said, "Surely the Spirit of God is in this man and his words are good. Can we find another who could more wisely manage the affairs of this kingdom than he?" And so it came about that Pharaoh made Joseph ruler over all the land of Egypt.

And Pharaoh clothed Joseph in royal robes and put a gold chain about his neck. He took his signet ring from off his hand and placed it upon Joseph's, and said, "You shall be overseer of my house, and your word shall govern my people in all the land of Egypt. Only in the throne will I be greater than you." And Pharaoh gave Joseph the second chariot that he had. In this Joseph rode through the streets of the city and the people bowed themselves before him. Pharaoh called Joseph, Zaphnath-paaneah, which means, "The man to whom secrets are revealed." He also gave Joseph an Egyptian princess for his wife.

All this prosperity did not change the heart of Joseph, for he remained kind and just to all. Day after day he rode

through the land and gathered up the food that grew every-where in abundance. This excess food he stored in buildings for future needs, until finally he had an enormous quantity laid aside for the years of famine.

During this time God blessed Joseph with two sons, whom he named Manasseh and Ephraim. And Joseph was grateful to God for all his blessings. He realized that all his troubles had brought about the great honor that he now enjoyed.

When the seven years of plenty had passed by, the years of trouble began. Nowhere in all the land of Egypt would the fields yield any growth, and people began to have need of food. Then they came to Joseph, and he opened the store-houses, which had been filled during the years of plenty, and sold food to the Egyptians.

Not only in Egypt did the terrible famine rage, but also in the countries round about. From far and near people came to Joseph, imploring him to sell corn to them lest they die of hunger.

Gen. 42

In the land of Canaan the deadly famine was making itself felt. Food was becoming scarce, and people were wondering what they should do. Then good news came that there was plenty of food in Egypt. Jacob and his eleven sons were rich in silver and gold and cattle. But without grain their riches could not keep them alive. So Jacob sent his ten eldest sons to Egypt to buy corn. He kept his youngest son, Benjamin, at home, because he loved

Benjamin the best of all after Joseph was taken away from him. He would never allow Benjamin to go far away from home lest some dreadful thing should happen to him also.

More than twenty years had now passed by since the ten brothers tore Joseph away from his father's loving care. During those years the brothers had grown more thoughtful of each other, and they did not envy Benjamin because he was loved the best. They were kind to him. No doubt they often thought about the terrible wrong they had done by selling Joseph.

Now, as they journeyed to Egypt, perhaps they remembered that the merchants who bought Joseph were going to that same country. And they may have passed along the very same road. But unpleasant thoughts are never cheerful traveling companions, and the brothers may have tried to think about other things. They saw new stretches of country before them and eagerly watched for the first glimpse of Egypt.

When they arrived in Egypt, things looked different from what they had expected. The fields were just as barren as those of Canaan. But they soon learned that although the famine was raging in Egypt, plenty of food was to be had there, for the great storehouses were filled with an abundance of corn. As every one who wished to buy food came to Joseph, they also came.

But the brothers did not know Joseph. More than twenty years had changed him from a mere lad into a full-grown man. Now he sat upon a throne, dressed like a prince, and every one who approached him with a request bowed humbly before him just as if he were the king. His ten brothers also bowed down before him, as the other people did.

Joseph knew his brothers at once, and when they bowed before him he remembered his dreams. Now he knew those dreams had come true, and he understood why God had permitted him to be sold into Egypt. He wished to know if his brothers had changed during the years that had passed. So he pretended that he did not know them. He spoke to them in the language of the Egyptian people and pretended to be stern and harsh.

"Who are you?" he demanded roughly.

They replied, "We are men of Canaan, and we are brothers."

"You are spies," he told them, "and I know you have come to see the stricken condition of our country. You wish to bring an army against us."

"Indeed we are not spies," they answered, "for we are true men, and we have come to buy food for ourselves and our families."

Joseph insisted that they were surely spies, and they told him again that they were brothers, the sons of one man.

"Is your father yet alive?" he asked, "and have you another brother?" What strange questions! they thought, and they told him about their aged father and about his tender love for Benjamin.

Now Joseph wondered whether they were kind to Benjamin. He also wondered if they cared more for their father's happiness than they did when they sold his son Joseph to the Ishmaelites. He thought, "I must find out these things before I let them know that I am Joseph." So he said, "You must prove to me that you are not spies. I will put nine of you into prison and the other one I will send back to Canaan. If he will return with the youngest brother of whom you told me, then I will believe that you are true men."

Into prison, where he had spent several long years, Joseph now placed his ten brothers; not because he hated them, but because he wished to know surely if they were now better men than they used to be. After three days he sent for them again, and said, "I fear God, and I want to do the right thing. If you are indeed true men you can prove it in this manner: I will send nine of you back to your aged father with food, and keep one of you in prison; you must return again and bring that younger brother of whom you spoke, or else I will know surely that you are spies.

The brothers felt at once that this great trouble had come upon them because they had been so unkind and cruel to their young brother Joseph. They did not know this man was Joseph, and that he could understand their language, so they said to each other, "We are suffering now because of our sin. Now we know how terrified Joseph felt when we sold him and when he pleaded with us, but we would not listen." Reuben, the eldest brother and the one who had wished to save Joseph's life, now spoke. "I told you then that you should not sin against the boy, and you would not hear me. Now his blood is being required at our hands."

Joseph pretended not to know what they were saying, but he heard it all and his heart was touched. Now he knew they were sorry for their sin, and he turned his face away and wept for joy. Then he dried his tears and spoke to them again in the language of the Egyptians. He took Simeon, who was the second eldest, and bound him before their eyes, and put him back into the prison. The others he sent away to Canaan, after their sacks had been filled with corn. He had commanded his servants to return their money in each sack with the corn.

On the homeward journey the brothers were sad at heart. What would their dear old father say, they wondered. Joseph was lost to him, and now Simeon was a prisoner, and Benjamin's presence was demanded in Egypt or else Simeon would be killed! No wonder they were sad. At the end of the first day they stopped to feed their donkeys, and one brother opened his sack and found his bag of money in it. More trouble seemed to be coming upon them; for they feared now that the stern ruler would believe they had stolen the money.

At last they reached home, tired and discouraged. They told their father about the sorrows that had befallen them and explained why Simeon was left in Egypt. "We cannot return again without Benjamin," they said.

"I can never let you take my youngest son," Jacob replied, "for Joseph is not, and Simeon is not, and now you will let some misfortune overtake Benjamin also."

Then the brothers emptied their sacks of food in the presence of their father, and found that each one's money had been replaced in his sack. Things seemed to be growing worse for them instead of better, and they were very much afraid.

Gen. 43:1–45:24

The famine continued to rage in Canaan; not a cloud appeared in the sky, and not a drop of dew sparkled on the parched grass. The waters of the brooks dried up, and the wells were becoming more shallow every day. After a while the food that Jacob's sons had brought from Egypt was nearly all eaten up. "You must go again," said Jacob, "and buy more corn."

But Judah answered, "We cannot go unless we take Benjamin; for the ruler told us we surely should not get any more corn if we failed to bring him."

"Why did you tell him that you had a younger brother?" Jacob asked.

Judah replied, "The man asked us whether we had yet another brother, and we only answered his questions. How could we tell that he would require us to bring him to Egypt?"

Still Jacob shook his head and refused to let Benjamin go; and the days dragged on and the food supply grew less and less. The brothers looked at each other sorrowfully and wondered what they should do. Although they were grown men, they did not dare leave their father on such an errand without his permission; for among those people the father ruled his household as long as he lived. And they could not go without Benjamin. Finally Judah said, "If you do not send us soon, both we and our children shall die of hunger; for, see, only a little food remains. I will certainly take care of Benjamin, and if any harm should befall him I will bear the blame forever." And Reuben, the eldest, had brought two of his own boys to Jacob, saying, "You may kill my sons if I do not bring Benjamin back safely."

At last, in the face of hunger and starvation, poor old Jacob was persuaded to send Benjamin with his brothers. "If my children must all be taken away from me, then I must bear the loss of them," he said.

Preparations began at once for this second journey. Jacob urged his sons to take for a present to the ruler some of the best things that grew in Canaan, and they selected some rich spices and perfumes, wild honey, and nuts. Then they took back twice as much money as on the first journey; for their father said that perhaps their money had been restored in their sacks by mistake.

When the brothers came into Joseph's presence the second time, and he saw that Benjamin had come with them, he sent them to his own house at once and gave orders to his servants to prepare a feast. "The men from Canaan are going to dine with me," he said to his steward, who was ruler of his house.

The brothers did not understand Joseph's orders to his servants, and they were frightened because they were brought to his own house. "He thinks we stole the money," they told each other, "and now although we are innocent he will accuse us of this wrong-doing and put us all into prison with Simeon. What shall we do?" They decided to tell the steward about their troubles.

"Do not be afraid," the steward said, when he heard their story, "because I had your money, and it must have been your father's God who gave you the treasure in your sacks." Then he gave them food for their donkeys and water to wash their feet. Afterward he brought Simeon out to them and told them that they were all invited to eat dinner with his master.

At noon Joseph came home to meet them. He spoke kindly to them and asked at once whether their father was still alive. How deeply interested he seemed to be in the dear old man they had left in Canaan! Next he turned to Benjamin and asked, "Is this the younger brother of whom you spoke?" When he knew that Benjamin was indeed his own brother, he said, "The Lord be gracious to you, my son." He longed to kiss Benjamin and embrace him at once, but he wished to learn more about his ten older brothers before he should let them know that he was Joseph. So he hurried out of the room to hide his tears, and then washed his face lest they should see that he had been weeping.

The brothers were beginning to feel more comfortable. They were glad to find Simeon well, and they hoped to be soon returning again to Canaan with food and with pleasant tidings for their anxious father. He would be glad to know the stern ruler had been kind to them this time. And he would be happy to see both Benjamin and Simeon return safe.

After the tables had been arranged, Joseph and his brothers entered the dining-hall. Other guests were present—possibly Egyptian officers. The brothers saw that three tables had been arranged—one where Joseph sat alone because he was the ruler, another where the Egyptians sat, and around the third table the brothers were assigned places according to their ages, beginning with Reuben. "How strange!" they thought, "for how can this man know which of us is older than his brother?" Joseph then sent food to them from his table, to each man a portion and to Benjamin five times as much as to the others. Perhaps he wished to see if they were as jealous of Benjamin as they had once been of their brother Joseph.

The meal ended pleasantly, and the brothers thought again of returning to their home. "Fill their sacks with corn as you did before," Joseph instructed the steward, "and put their money back into the sacks again. But in Benjamin's sack put my silver cup also." And the steward did as he was bidden.

On the following morning the brothers started for home. But they had not gone far when the steward came hurrying after them. Joseph had sent him to recover the silver cup. "Why have you rewarded my master evil for good?" he asked when he told them that Joseph's cup was missing from the house.

"God forbid that we should be guilty of stealing the cup," they answered, "for we are honest men. Did we not return the money that we found in our sacks? Why then should your master think us guilty of this offense?"

So sure were they that none of them had done the wicked deed of which they were accused that they said, "Search us and see for yourself: if the cup is found, let that one die in whose sack it is discovered, and the others of us will become your servants."

The steward was unwilling to render such severe punishment. "If I find the cup," said he, "I will take him for my servant in whose sack it is found, and the others may go free."

Then the search began. Every man lowered his sack to

the ground and opened it for the steward's examination. And one by one the men rejoiced when the missing cup was not found in their possession. The steward began the search with Reuben's sack, and ended with Benjamin's. And in Benjamin's sack he found the missing cup, where he had placed it.

How astonished the brothers were at this discovery! What could they do now? Surely someone was trying to bring back the ill will of the ruler upon them. They could not part with Benjamin, and yet they had promised the steward he might take that one of them for a servant who should be guilty of such an offense. Tearing their clothes as an expression of grief, they replaced the sacks upon their donkeys and turned back to the capital city with Joseph's steward and Benjamin.

Joseph was waiting at his house for their coming. "What is this you have done?" he demanded, sternly, as they fell on their faces before him.

"Alas, God is punishing us for our sins. We are all your servants," exclaimed Judah.

"God forbid that I should keep all of you," answered Joseph, more kindly now; "only he who took the missing cup will I punish, and the others may return home." Joseph wished to see if the others were selfish and willing to let Benjamin suffer if they could escape.

Then Judah, who had promised Jacob to bring Benjamin safely back to Canaan or else bear the blame forever, fell on his face at Joseph's feet.

"Please do not be angry with me, but listen to my words," he said, "for I know you are even as Pharaoh. When we came at the first you asked whether we had a father or a younger brother and we told you that we had. We told you about our father's tender love for Benjamin after his favorite son had been lost. Then you demanded us to bring Benjamin with us when we should return again to prove that we are not spies. We replied that our father would not be willing to let him come because he feared some terrible harm might befall him, too. Still you insisted that unless we bring him we should never see your face again.

"When we returned home we told our father about your words, and he was grieved. He said he would not allow Benjamin to leave him. But when the food supply grew low, he wished to send us again, and we answered that we could not come and see you except Benjamin be with us. Then after some days of delaying he sent us again, saying, 'If trouble happen to Benjamin, I shall die of grief.' Now, if we return without the lad our father will die, for he is old and feeble and his life is bound up in his love for Benjamin. Let him return, I beg of you, and let me remain in his stead, for I promised our father that if ill should befall the lad I would bear the blame forever."

Judah's earnest words touched Joseph's heart deeply. How different they sounded from the words he spoke so long ago when he suggested to his brothers that they sell Joseph to the Ishmaelites! Now he was offering himself to become a lifetime slave in place of his younger brother; now he was pleading for the relief of his father's anxiety. A changed Judah, indeed. And Joseph knew that Judah's words were sincere; he believed his brothers were better men; and he longed to embrace them all. So he quickly commanded his Egyptian servants to leave the room, and then, turning to his brothers, he said in their language, "I am your brother Joseph; does my father yet live?"

Surprise and fear overcame the brothers and they could not answer a word. Joseph saw they were afraid, and he wept aloud and called them to come nearer. "I am the same Joseph you sold into Egypt," he told them, "but do not be afraid, nor angry with yourselves, because it was God who sent me here before you to save your lives. This terrible famine will continue for five more years, and you must bring your families and all your possessions into Egypt, or else you may die. I will take care of you here; for God has made me a father even to Pharaoh and the ruler of all his people." Then Joseph kissed Benjamin and embraced him fondly, and each of the brothers he kissed with the same forgiving tenderness.

The Egyptian servants heard Joseph weeping, and they hurried to tell Pharaoh that Joseph's brothers had come, and everyone was glad, because everyone loved Joseph. Pharaoh sent a message to Joseph, urging him to bring his father to Egypt at once.

The homeward journey was begun the second time, and now the men were taking Egyptian wagons loaded with good things to eat. Joseph sent as a present to his father twenty donkeys loaded with food and other stuff, and to each of his brothers he gave Egyptian clothing. To Benjamin he gave five times as much as he gave to the other ten, and also three hundred pieces of silver.

Gen. 45:25–50:26

The days of anxious waiting seemed long to Jacob as he watched for the homecoming of his sons from Egypt. At last they came with their treasures from Egypt— wagonloads of good things.

Jacob's joy was greatest when he saw Benjamin and Simeon among the stalwart men who came to give him an affectionate greeting. They told him at once of the good fortune that had overtaken them in Egypt. "We found Joseph!" they exclaimed excitedly, "and he is alive and well. More than that, he is the ruler of all Egypt, and he has sent us to bring you and our wives and sons and daughters to live in Egypt."

At first Jacob could not believe their words, for it seemed impossible that the son whom he had mourned as dead for more than twenty years should be alive in a strange land. But when he saw the wagons Joseph had sent and the twenty donkeys loaded with provisions as a special present to him, he said, "It is enough; Joseph my son is yet alive, and I will go and see him before I die."

The third journey to Egypt was a happy one. Jacob and his sons' wives and their little children rode in the wagons Joseph had sent, while the grown men drove the herds of cattle and sheep and goats and donkeys. One night they made camp at Beersheba, where Abraham and Isaac had lived long before this time. Here Jacob offered sacrifices to God as his father and grandfather had done. And God spoke to him once more in a night vision. "Do not be afraid to go to Egypt," God told him, "for I will go with you and will increase your family until they become a great nation. Then I will bring them again into the land that I promised to your grandfather Abraham and to your father Isaac. And you shall indeed see Joseph, and he will place his hand upon your eyes."

After this time Jacob was called Israel, the name that God gave him when he wrestled all night with the angel. And his children were called Israelites. But sometimes they were called Hebrews, a word that means, "From beyond the river," and it referred back to the long-ago time when their forefather Abraham had obeyed God's voice and had crossed the River Euphrates to journey to Canaan. When the Israelites came into Egypt they numbered sixty-seven people, and when Joseph and his two sons were counted among them they numbered seventy.

At the border-land of Egypt the Israelites camped again, and waited until Judah should go to Joseph to tell of their coming. Joseph prepared his royal chariot and rode into Goshen to meet his father and his relatives.

What a happy meeting when Father and son were clasped in each others' arms again! Both wept for joy and spoke many tender words to each other. Then Joseph brought five of his brothers and his aged father to see Pharaoh, the king.

Pharaoh was glad to see them. When he learned that they were shepherds, he told them they might live in the land of Goshen. Goshen lay between Egypt and the desert, and was in ordinary times a very fertile country because its soil was well watered by the broad River Nile. Joseph provided food for his relatives and for their herds during the remaining years of the famine.

After a while the Egyptian people spent all their money for food. Then they came to Joseph for more corn, and he said, "I will give you corn if you will sell your cattle to Pharaoh." This they did. Then when their cattle were sold and their money was spent their food supply again grew low. "What must we do now?" they asked Joseph, and he told them to sell their fields and their pastures to the king. And so after a while Pharaoh owned all the land in Egypt except the land that belonged to the priests. By and by the people became hungry again, and they had nothing left to sell except themselves. So they came to Joseph and said, "We would rather sell ourselves to become servants of Pharaoh than die of hunger." And they became servants of the king.

When the seven years of awful famine had passed by, Joseph sent the Egyptian farmers back to the fields with seed to plant again. He told them to plant their crops and care for them just as they had done before. Then when the harvest-time should come they should bring one-fifth of the yield of their fields to Pharaoh, and four-fifths they could keep for food and for seed for the coming year. "All the land belongs to Pharaoh," he said, "and hereafter one-fifth of all that grows on the land shall be kept for his portion." And these words of Joseph's became a law throughout all Egypt.

After the famine ended, Joseph's people continued to live in Goshen. Israel was one hundred and thirty years old when he left Canaan, and he lived seventeen years in Goshen. Before he died he called his sons and requested them to take his body to Canaan and bury it in the cave of Machpelah, where Abraham and Isaac were buried. Then he gave each of his sons a parting blessing.

Joseph brought his two children, Manasseh and Ephraim, to see their aged grandfather and to receive his blessing also. And Israel said, "Surely God has been good to me, for I thought I should never see your face again and now I am permitted to see both you and your children." He then placed his trembling, wrinkled hands upon the boys' heads to bless them. Joseph saw he had placed his right hand upon the head of Ephraim, the younger, and his left hand upon the head of Manasseh. "Not so, my father," he said gently, trying to lift his father's hands and change them so that the right hand should rest upon Manasseh's head. But Israel would not allow the change. "I know what I am doing," he answered, "although I am feeble and my eyes are dim; your younger son shall become greater than the elder, and to him the greater blessing belongs." Israel also gave each of the boys a portion among the inheritance of his own children.

After Israel died, Joseph commanded the Egyptian physicians to embalm his father's body for burial. This required forty days' time. In all, the people spent seventy days mourning the death of this aged man. Then Joseph asked permission of Pharaoh to go with his brothers to place Israel's body in the burial cave in Canaan.

When they returned again to Goshen, the brothers thought, "Perhaps Joseph has been kind to us only for our father's sake, and now he may treat us cruelly because we sinned against him so long ago." So they sent a messenger to Joseph, saying, "Your father before he died asked that you forgive the wrong-doing of your brothers, and now we beg that you do forgive us, for we are servants of the God of your father." The messenger delivered the request of the brothers to Joseph.

Joseph wept when he heard this message. He knew his brothers feared that he might harm them, now that their father had died. So he called them to him and said, "Do not be afraid of me. Am I in the place of God that I should attempt to punish you because of your sin? No; I will care for you and for your children as long as I live." His kind words comforted their hearts, and they believed that he had indeed freely forgiven them.

As the years passed by, Joseph's relatives increased in number until they became a strong nation. And Joseph cared for them as long as he lived. When he reached the age of one hundred and ten years he knew his time had come to die. He called the old men of Israel to his bedside and said, "I am going to die. But God will watch over you, and by and by he will lead you back to the land of your fathers. Do not bury me here in Egypt, but place my body in a coffin and take it back with you when you return to Canaan." And the men of Israel wept as they promised to show this kindness to the one who had been so good to them. Afterward whenever they looked at Joseph's coffin they remembered his words, and they knew they should not always live in Egypt.

THE STORY OF MOSES AND THE ISRAELITES

Exodus 1:1–2:10

Our stories about the Bible patriarchs, such as were Abraham, Isaac, and Jacob, are now ended, and we are beginning the good stories about one of the most interesting persons in the Old Testament. This person is Moses.

You remember that Jacob, the last of the patriarchs, was called Israel, and that his children were called Israelites. These Israelites lived in the land of Goshen for a long time after their fathers who brought them from Canaan had died. And they grew in numbers until they became a strong nation.

During this time Pharaoh, the king who had been kind to Joseph and to his kinsmen, died too, and another Pharaoh took his place upon the Egyptian throne. This new

Pharaoh did not look kindly upon the fast-growing nation of Israelites. He thought, "Soon these people will number more than my own Egyptian people, and they may join themselves with our enemies who come to fight against us. Then they will go away from our country and we can no longer have them for our servants. I cannot let them go away from Goshen; I must keep them for slaves."

Pharaoh called his people together and told them of his fears concerning the Israelites. "We must do something," he said, "to hinder them from becoming stronger and more powerful than we are." Finally he and his officers decided to make the Israelites work harder than they had ever worked before. Pharaoh wished to have new cities built, where he could store his rich treasures, and he commanded the Israelites to build those cities. Then the officers placed taskmasters over the workmen to compel them to work very hard and very fast. But the harder they worked the stronger they grew, and Pharaoh saw that his plan was not a success. "This will never do," he reasoned, "for the Israelites are growing stronger all the while I afflict them. I must make life even more miserable for them." And he did.

The hard-working Israelites were horror-stricken when one morning this message came to them from the king's house: "Every baby boy that is born among your people must be thrown into the River Nile." Because this was the king's command it had to be obeyed.

After this cruel command had been put into practice, one day baby Moses was born. Now, his mother feared God, and she believed it was very wicked to throw a child into the river. Like all mothers, she loved her baby; and for three months she hid him. When she could hide him no longer she thought of a wise plan, and then she worked carefully to carry it out. First she gathered some bulrushes—plants that grew along the River's bank—then she wove a little ark-like basket, and plastered it well with lime and pitch so that no water could leak through. When this was finished, she made a soft bed in the ark and placed her baby in it. Now the very hardest part remained to be done; but she was a brave woman and she believed God would help her save the baby's life. So she carried the basket to the river, and there among the tall reeds that grew near the water's edge she placed her precious burden, and went away. Her little daughter Miriam, who had come along, lingered near the bank to play and to watch what should happen to the tiny ark. She had not long to wait, for soon a company of richly dressed women came to the river's bank. One of them was the Egyptian princess, Pharaoh's daughter. They had come to bathe in the river.

When the princess saw the strange-looking ark floating among the reeds, she sent her maid to bring it ashore. "What can be inside this queer basket?" the women wondered as they gathered round to see it opened. And how surprised they were when a sweet-faced baby looked up at them and cried.

The princess knew about the cruel command her father had given, and she said at once, "This is one of the Israelite's children." She was more kind-hearted than her wicked father, and she wished to spare this baby's life. So she decided to take him for her own son. Just then a little Israelite girl came running along the bank. She heard the princess say about the little baby, "I shall keep him for my own son." This little girl was Miriam, and her heart was glad because she knew her baby brother could live. Bravely she stepped up to the princess and said, "Shall I go and call an Israelite woman to nurse this baby for you?" Of course there would need to be a nurse, and the princess was quite willing to hire an Israelite woman, so Miriam hurried home and quickly brought her own mother. And they carried the baby back once more to their own home, where they should no longer need to fear that its cries might attract the attention of their enemies, for every one learned that this baby had been adopted by the King's daughter.

When the baby grew old enough to leave his mother, he was taken to Pharaoh's palace and given to the Princess. She called his name Moses, which means, "drawn out," because she had drawn him out of the water. And she placed him in the best schools of Egypt, that he might learn all the wisdom of her own people and be ready some day to occupy the Egyptian throne.

Exod. 2:11-25

When the boy Moses grew to manhood he did not forget his own people—the Israelites. Sometimes he left the beautiful palace and its gardens, where he lived among the princes of Egypt, and went out to the fields and cities where his people were toiling. His heart felt sad when he saw the cruel taskmasters oppress his people. He believed that God had spared his life when he was a baby in order that he might some day help his own people. How he longed for that time to come!

One day Moses, when he had left the king's palace to visit the Israelites, acted very unwisely. He saw an Egyptian beating an Israelite, and this made him very angry. He looked about quickly to see that no one was watching, and then he killed the Egyptian and buried him in the sand. He thought the Israelite would understand that he was trying to help him. The next day he saw two Israelites quarreling between themselves and beginning to fight. "Why are you so unkind to each other?" he asked, and the one who had done the wrong replied crossly, "Who made you a ruler and a judge over us? Do you intend to kill me as you killed the Egyptian yesterday?"

When Moses heard these words he understood at once that his people did not expect him to help them. They did not know how much he loved them and how greatly he desired to relieve their burdens. They were not keeping the secret of his act the day before, and soon Pharaoh would hear of the Egyptian's death. Then Pharaoh would be angry with Moses and would seek to kill him. Knowing this, Moses hurried away from his people with a sad heart, and sought a hiding place in the wilderness.

After a long, tiresome journey across the desert, Moses one day came to a well. Here he sat down to rest. Presently seven young women came to the well to draw water. They were sisters, and they kept their father's flocks. While they were drawing water for the sheep some wicked shepherds came by and tried to drive them away. Many times before those wicked shepherds had annoyed the young women. But this time Moses defended the women and compelled the wicked shepherds to go away.

When the sisters returned home with the flocks, their father, Jethro, who was a priest of Midian, asked, "How is it that you have come home so early today?" "We met a stranger at the well," they replied, "who helped us when the wicked men tried to drive our sheep away." Jethro then sent for Moses and invited him to live among his people, and to care for his flocks. Later he gave one of his daughters to become Moses' wife, and for many years Moses worked as a shepherd in the land of Midian. Because he was a stranger among the people of Midian, Moses named his eldest son Gershom, which means, "A stranger here."

During this time a change had taken place in Egypt. The Pharaoh, whom Moses feared, had died, and a new Pharaoh had come to the Egyptian throne. This ruler was just as cruel as the one whose place he took. Daily he oppressed the Israelites and added miseries to their unhappy lives. As they worked and toiled their hearts grew very sad. They groaned beneath their heavy burdens, and they wept and prayed for relief. And God heard their prayers.

You remember that long before this time God promised to give the land of Canaan to the children of Abraham, Isaac, and Jacob. You remember, too, that Jacob's name was changed to Israel, and that his children and their children after them were called Israelites. And so it was these Israelites to whom God had promised the land of Canaan. Now when God heard their cries of distress in Egypt he remembered his promise to Abraham, Isaac, and Israel. And he planned to deliver them from Pharaoh's cruel bondage and bring them to their own land.

Although forty years had passed since Moses fled out of

Egypt, still one of the Israelites remembered that Moses had believed God would some day use him to help his people. This Israelite was Moses' brother, Aaron. Now Aaron, too, had believed that God spared the life of Moses when he was a baby in order to use him some day as a deliverer for his oppressed kinsmen. But Moses was gone far away now, and Aaron thought he might have forgotten about the suffering of his people.

One day Aaron decided to go out into the great wilderness to search for his lost brother. "If I find him," he thought, "I shall tell him that the king whom he knew and feared is dead, and that the new Pharaoh has been equally as cruel to our people as the one whose place he took. When Moses hears about the suffering of our people, surely he will try to help us." But Aaron did not realize what a changed Moses he should find.

Exod. 3–4

When Aaron started out from Goshen to search in the wilderness for his lost brother, Moses was leading his flock to a green pasture near the foot of Mount Horeb. How different Moses looked now from the young man who had once lived in Pharaoh's palace! No longer he wore the princely robes of Egypt. Now his dress was the coarse mantle of a shepherd, and he carried a long shepherd's staff, or rod, in his hand. Day after day and year after year he had cared for his father-in-law's sheep, leading them to fresh pasture lands and to abundant water supplies. The sun and the wind had tanned his face and hands, while the years had whitened his flowing hair.

Although when a young man Moses had learned all the wisdom of the Egyptians until he became one of the greatest persons the world has ever known, he did not think himself great, nor wise. He was contented to fill the humble place of a shepherd. He was glad to live in the great wilderness, far away from the large cities and beautiful grounds of Pharaoh's palace. Here he could see all around him the wonderful things that God had made. He learned much about that country—its pasture lands and watering places. He often studied the trees and bushes and flowers. Because he was interested in these things, God spoke to him one day from a bush.

The sheep were feeding on the rich pasture and Moses was looking about at the beauties and wonders of nature when presently he saw a flame of fire burst forth from a bush on the mountainside. He watched, expecting to see the bush destroyed by the fire; but the flame kept burning, and no harm came to the bush. "What a strange sight!" thought Moses; "I must take a closer look at this unusual bush, which fire cannot harm." As he started forward, he heard a voice speak to him from the flame. "Moses! Moses!" the voice called; and Moses replied, "Here am I."

"Do not come near the bush," the voice said. "Put off the shoes from your feet, for you are standing on holy ground."

Moses understood at once that God was speaking to him; for the people in those lands always remove their shoes when they approach a sacred place, and perhaps Moses had done likewise when he stood before an altar to worship God.

So he stooped down quickly to loosen and remove his sandals. Then he hid his face, for he was afraid to look upon the flame again.

"I am the God of Abraham, of Isaac, and of Jacob," the voice began once more, "and I have seen the afflictions of my people, the Israelites, in Egypt. I have heard their cries, and I know their sorrows. Now I am come to deliver them from the Egyptians and to bring them into the land that I promised to their fathers."

No doubt Moses was glad to hear this good news, for he still loved his own people. He had thought of them many times as he led his flock to and fro across the desert plains. How like a flock were they, in the hands of a cruel shepherd!

But the voice continued to speak: "Come now, and I will send you to Pharaoh, that you may bring my people out of Egypt."

Although when a young man Moses had expected some day to rescue his people from Pharaoh's cruel oppression, now he did not feel himself great enough to undertake such a task. "Who am I," he asked the Lord, "that I should bring my people out of Egypt? This is too great a work for me to do."

"I will go with you and help do the great work," answered the voice from the flame. "And when you bring the Israelites to this mountain, where they shall serve me, then you shall know that certainly I have been with you."

Moses feared that his people would not believe God had sent him to be their deliverer. He said, "When I go to the Israelites and tell them you have sent me, it may be they will have forgotten you. If they ask, 'Who is this

God?' what shall I say?"

And God said, "Tell them that my name is I AM, the One who is always living. And tell them that I AM has sent you to help them. Do not be afraid, for they will believe you. Then call together the elders of your families, who are the leaders of your people, and go with them to Pharaoh and tell him, 'Our God, the God of the Hebrews, the Israelites, has met us, and now let us go three days' journey into the wilderness to worship him.' At first the king will refuse to let you go; but after I have shown my power in Egypt he will send you out of the land."

Still Moses was fearful that his people would not believe God had sent him except he could show them some sign, for a proof. So he asked God to give him such a sign, and God said to him. "What is that in your hand?"

"It is a rod," answered Moses.

God told him to throw the rod on the ground, and Moses obeyed. Instantly the rod was turned into a snake, and when Moses saw it he was afraid, and ran from it.

But God said, "Do not be afraid; but take hold of its tail."

Moses obeyed again, and the snake became once more a rod in his hand.

Then God told Moses to put his hand into his bosom, under his mantle, and take it out again. When Moses did so his hand was changed until it became like the hand of a leper, white as snow and covered with a scaly crust. Moses was frightened, because leprosy is a dreadful disease. But God said, "Put your hand into your bosom once more," and when Moses obeyed his hand became like the other, with a healthy skin. God intended that Moses could use this sign for a second proof to his people and to the Egyptians that God had sent him. God further told Moses that if they should refuse to believe both these signs he was to take water from the river and pour it upon the ground before them. This water God would cause to turn into blood, and this would be the third sign.

Moses still felt unwilling to go. He told God that he could not speak well, and asked God to choose someone else for the work. But God had chosen Moses for the work, and he said to Moses, "Am I not the Lord, who made man's mouth? Go, and I will teach you what to say."

When Moses continued to ask that someone else should go in his stead, God said, "I will send your brother, Aaron, with you, and he will speak the words you tell him to speak. Even now he is coming into the wilderness to meet you."

At last Moses was ready to obey God. He led his flock back to Jethro, his father-in-law, and said, "Let me return to my people in Egypt, and see if they are yet alive." And Jethro said, "Go in peace."

God spoke again to Moses in the land of Midian, and told him that those who had sought his life in Egypt were now dead. Then Moses took his wife and sons and started toward the land of Goshen, carrying in his hand the rod through which God had performed a miracle. On his way he met Aaron, and together the two brothers returned to Egypt.

Moses told Aaron all the words God had spoken to him and the signs God had given. Then they called the elders of Israel and told them that God had sent Moses to be their deliverer. When the people heard the words of the Lord and saw the signs God had given, they believed and were glad. Then they bowed their heads and worshiped God because he had heard their prayers.

Exod. 5:1–7:24

One day a messenger came to Pharaoh saying, "Two men, who are Israelites, stand outside wishing to speak with you."

"Bring them in," said the King; and the messenger soon returned with Moses and Aaron.

Moses had not forgotten how to behave himself in the king's house even though he had spent long years in the wilderness among common people. He and Aaron spoke to Pharaoh and told him that the Lord God of the Israelites had said, "Let my people go, that they may worship me in the wilderness."

But Pharaoh answered, "Who is the Lord, that I should obey his voice?" Because he was ruler of the great land of Egypt, Pharaoh was too proud to believe there was a higher Power, who could give orders for him to obey. "I do not know the Lord," he said, "and I shall not let Israel go out of my country to worship him."

Moses and Aaron then told Pharaoh that the God of the Hebrews had met with them, and that unless his people were given freedom to go on a three days' journey into the wilderness to serve him there with sacrifices, he would send terrible diseases upon them and kill them.

These words did not move Pharaoh's hard heart in the least. He only frowned, and replied crossly, "Why are you trying to take the people away from their work? I know they are idle, or they would not be asking to go away to sacrifice to their God. Return now, both of you, to your tasks, and let the Israelites alone." And with these words he sent Moses and Aaron out of his court.

On that same day Pharaoh called the taskmasters and commanded that they should make the Israelites work harder than they had ever worked before. At this time they were making bricks and building houses for the rulers of Egypt. In mixing the clay for the bricks they were using straw, chopped up fine, to hold the clay together. Every day the Egyptians brought straw for their work. Now Pharaoh commanded that no straw should be brought to them. "Send them out into the fields to gather straw for themselves," said he, "and see that they make just as many bricks as on other days when straw was brought to them."

Now, instead of getting freedom from Pharaoh's cruel bondage, the Israelites were having greater trouble than ever. Of course they could not gather straw from the fields and still make as many bricks as before; and when their work fell short they were beaten by the task-masters. At once they blamed Moses and Aaron for their trouble. "You promised to bring us out of Egypt, and you are only bringing more sorrow upon us," they said.

Moses loved his people and he pitied them. He cried to the Lord, and said, "Why is it that you sent me to Pharaoh? He will not let the people go, and he is making life more miserable for them."

God spoke comforting words to Moses and sent him to encourage the Israelites; but they were in such deep sorrow that they would not listen to Moses. Then God said, "Go in and speak to Pharaoh again, and show him the signs I have given you." But Moses answered, "How can I go when the Israelites no longer believe you have sent me? Neither will Pharaoh hear my words."

Moses was ready to give up because Pharaoh would not let the people go at once. He did not understand how God was planning to work mighty signs and wonders in Egypt until all the Egyptians should fear Israel's God. Then the Lord told him to return again and again to Pharaoh and perform great miracles before him. "I have made you as a god to Pharaoh," the Lord said, "and Aaron shall be your prophet. Because of this Pharaoh will hear your words, even though he refuses to obey me."

After this Moses took Aaron and went the second time to talk with Pharaoh. And Pharaoh asked them to show him a sign, or miracle, that he might know the God of the Hebrews had surely sent them.

Now Aaron had in his hand the rod that Moses brought from the wilderness. Moses told him to cast this rod down before Pharaoh and before his servants. Aaron did so, and the rod became a snake. Pharaoh knew this was a miracle. But he had in his court some wise men called sorcerers, or magicians, and they also claimed to work miracles. Pharaoh sent for them, and when they came they too threw their rods before him. And their rods became snakes. But Aaron's rod swallowed up their rods and afterward became a harmless cane in Aaron's hand again.

Even when Pharaoh knew that his magicians could not work so great a miracle as could Moses and Aaron, still he would not listen to them nor believe their sign, and they went away the second time from his presence.

On the next morning God sent Moses and Aaron to speak to Pharaoh again. This time they met him on the bank of the River Nile. Perhaps the king was surprised to see these aged men approach him. Perhaps he felt angry because they were disturbing him so often. But Moses and Aaron were not afraid. They knew God had sent them and they spoke boldly to the king. "Because you refuse to let the Israelites go," they began, "the Lord our God has sent us to you once more. Now he has commanded us to show you another sign." Then Moses spoke to Aaron, and he waved his rod over the waters of the great river. At that very moment the water became blood. Then all the fishes died, and soon a dreadful odor filled the air. Aaron stretched his rod toward the waters of the rivers and streams and lakes and ponds, and everywhere throughout the land of Egypt the water became blood.

Pharaoh's magicians brought to him water in a vessel and changed it into blood. Then the king turned away and went back to his palace But the Egyptian people grew alarmed, because they had no water to drink. Nowhere in all the land could they find a drop of water.

Exod. 7:25–10:29

A full week passed by before God lifted the terrible plague of blood from the waters of Egypt. Then he sent Moses and Aaron to tell Pharaoh that another terrible plague was coming. This time when Aaron, at God's command, stretched his rod over the rivers and lakes and ponds, frogs came hopping up out of the water in great numbers and covered all the land. They went into the people's houses, and even into Pharaoh's palace, and hopped onto the beds and into the cooking vessels. The magicians tried, and they, too, brought frogs up out of the water.

Pharaoh was greatly troubled. He had been too stubborn to let any one know how much the plague of blood had annoyed him. But now the frogs worried him very much. When he could endure them no longer he called for Moses and Aaron and begged them to ask God to take the frogs away. "I will let your people go to sacrifice to the Lord," he promised; and Moses asked, "When do you want God to destroy the frogs out of your houses?" Pharaoh answered, "Tomorrow."

Moses prayed, and on the next day frogs died everywhere, except in the river. The Egyptians gathered them out of the houses and from the fields and piled them up in great heaps.

But when the frogs were gone Pharaoh did not keep his promise. He grew stubborn again, and refused to let the people go. Then God sent another plague. This time Aaron struck his rod upon the dust of the ground, and the dust became lice and fleas. The magicians tried, but they could not perform this miracle. They told Pharaoh that God's power was greater than theirs. Still Pharaoh would not listen. How hard his heart was growing!

Then God sent Moses and Aaron to the king again as he walked along the river's bank early one morning. "Because you will not let Israel go," they told him, "tomorrow God will send another plague upon your land. Great swarms of flies will fill your palace and the houses of your servants. Everywhere—indoors and out-of-doors, the flies will trouble you. But no flies will enter the houses of the Israelites in Goshen."

When the swarms of flies came upon the Egyptians, Pharaoh called for Moses and Aaron again. "Tell your people to sacrifice to their God in Goshen," he said.

But Moses replied, "They must go away out of the land, for the Egyptians would stone them if they should see their sacrifices." The Egyptians worshiped oxen, and the Israelites killed oxen and sacrificed them on the altars that they built to worship God. The Egyptians would be very angry if they should see the Israelites kill oxen to sacrifice, because they believed oxen were sacred, or holy animals.

When Moses refused Pharaoh's offer to let the Israelites worship in Goshen, the King said, "I will let them go to the wilderness, only do not take them very far away."

Moses answered, "We must go three days' journey; and you must not break your promise to God, for he is a terrible God when once he is angry and he will surely punish you for your wickedness."

But just as soon as God removed the plague of flies in

answer to Moses' prayer, Pharaoh grew stubborn again and refused to let the Israelites go.

The next great plague that God sent upon the land of Egypt affected the cattle, and horses, and camels, and oxen, and sheep. Many of the cattle in Egypt died of this great plague, and Pharaoh became alarmed. But when he sent a messenger down to Goshen he learned that the Israelites' cattle were all alive and well. Even after this Pharaoh remained stubborn.

God kept telling Moses what to do next, and so the sixth plague came when Moses sprinkled a handful of dust in the air before Pharaoh. Boils now broke out upon the people of Egypt. Dreadful boils they were, and painful. Because of them the magicians could not stand before Pharaoh. Still the king remained stubborn, and unwilling to obey God. Then Moses warned him that the greatest trouble he had ever seen in Egypt should come the next day if he still refused to let the people go. The people were warned to seek shelter for themselves and for their beasts lest they should be killed by this terrible plague. Some of the Egyptians had learned to believe Moses and Aaron, and they hurried to their homes. But others, like Pharaoh, were not willing to listen to the warning, and they remained in their fields.

When the sky grew black with storm clouds and the thunder began to peal, the people became afraid. It seldom rains in Egypt, and they had never heard thunder nor seen lightning before. Soon the hail stones began to fall as fast as raindrops, and the lightning ran like fire along the ground. All living things that had remained in the fields were killed by the lightning and hail.

Now Pharaoh was terribly frightened. He called loudly for Moses and Aaron to come at once. And he cried out, "I have sinned this time; I and my people are wicked." He promised that the Israelites might go at once if God would only cause the awful thunder and lightning and hail storm to cease. Moses answered, "I will spread out my hands toward heaven as soon as I am outside the city, and the storm will cease, that you may know the earth belongs to God. But I know that you and your people do not yet fear the Lord God as you should fear him."

When the storm clouds rolled away, Pharaoh looked out upon the bright sunlight again and his heart grew as hard as before. He was not at all willing to obey God.

Moses may have grown tired of going so often to the king. But God told him that more plagues should yet come upon Egypt before Pharaoh would really let the Israelites get out of the land of Goshen. The hail storm had destroyed all the growing crops in the land, but the wheat and rye were not damaged because they had not grown up. The next plague, God told Moses, would be locusts, and they would eat up every green thing that appeared above the ground. When the Egyptians heard that another plague was coming upon the land they hurried to Pharaoh and said, "How long are you going to let these men bother our country? The land is spoiled already by the hail, and if the locusts come they will destroy everything."

So Pharaoh called Moses and Aaron and asked, "Whom do you intend to take with you when you go to worship your God?"

Moses replied, "We will take all of our people, and we

will also take our flocks and herds."

"Take only your men and let them sacrifice," Pharaoh said, and, refusing to hear Moses' reply, he drove them from his presence.

When Moses went out from Pharaoh's palace, the Lord said, "Stretch out your hand over the land of Egypt for the locusts to come," and Moses obeyed. Then an east wind began to blow. All that day and all the next night the east wind blew, and when morning came again a great cloud of locusts appeared in the sky. They covered the whole land of Egypt, and were so many that they darkened the land.

Fear came into Pharaoh's heart again, and he sent in haste for Moses and Aaron. "I have sinned against the Lord your God, and against you," he said. "Now forgive me this time, and pray that God will take these locusts away, or I and my people shall die." And Moses prayed again, and the Lord sent a strong west wind, which carried the locusts away and drowned them in the Red Sea.

When Pharaoh hardened his heart again, God told Moses to stretch his hand out toward heaven once more, and this time a great darkness would come upon the land of Egypt. Moses did so, and a thick darkness covered the land. For three days there was no light at all in Egypt—not even moonlight nor starlight.

Pharaoh sent the last time for Moses and Aaron, and said, "I will let all the people go as you have asked; only they must not take their flocks and herds."

But Moses answered boldly, "We shall take with us everything that we have when we go to serve our God."

Now Pharaoh became very angry, and he said, "Get out

of my sight. And if I ever see your face again I shall kill you."

Moses answered bravely, "It shall be just as you say; for you shall never see my face again. But know this: God will send one more terrible plague upon you and your people, after which the Israelites will go away out of your land." And so saying he walked out of the Egyptian court.

Exod. 11–13

Evening shadows were beginning to creep over the land of Goshen and across the barren fields of Egypt. Everything had grown quiet around the walls and buildings where the Israelites had toiled. Never again would the men return to pick up their tools and work for Pharaoh. The time had come when they were going to leave Goshen.

Before this God had told Moses that one more plague was coming upon Pharaoh and upon Egypt. So terrible should it be that Pharaoh would want to drive the Israelites out of the land. "Tell the people to get ready to leave quickly," the Lord had said; "for they must start at once when Pharaoh's messenger comes."

And the Israelites believed now that God had sent Moses to help them. They honored him as a great man, indeed, and were ready to obey him because they saw the wonders that God brought upon Egypt through Moses' words. Many of the Egyptians, too, honored Moses as a great man, and became friendly toward the Israelites. They even seemed eager to please the people whom they once hated and scorned as slaves. They had seen how God protected his people from the troubles that came upon Egypt.

On this evening every household in Goshen was very busy. Instead of preparing for a restful night of sleep, every man, woman, and child was wide awake and very much excited about something. They were obeying the command that Moses had given them from God. Every father was killing a lamb and sprinkling blood upon the door frame of his dwelling. Every mother was preparing vegetables to cook with the roasted lamb. Every boy and girl was helping to gather the flocks and herds from the scattered pasture-lands of Goshen, or to run errands for his parents.

"Tonight at midnight," Moses had said, "God will send an angel through the land, and every house where blood is not sprinkled upon the door frame this angel will enter. And he will bring death to the eldest child in that home." Moses told the Israelites to kill a lamb for each family, and sprinkle their door frames with blood. "Then," said Moses, "roast the lamb and with it cook vegetables, and prepare for a midnight supper. For when the death-angel passes over the land you must be dressed and ready to start on a journey. You must eat your supper standing around the table. Neither shall any of you go out into the darkness, lest the angel meet you there and you die."

This midnight supper was called the "Pass-over" supper, because the angel passed over the houses of the Israelites when he saw their blood-sprinkled door frames. And God commanded that the Israelites should eat such a supper once each year, at the same time, in memory of the night when he kept them from death in Egypt.

Now, the Egyptians did not sprinkle blood on their door

frames, nor prepare a midnight meal. Every one of them had gone to bed as usual, expecting to sleep soundly until the next daydawn. But at midnight they were awakened. Even Pharaoh was aroused. He hurried to the bedside of his eldest son—and found him dead. What a terrible plague! Pharaoh knew God had done this, and he cried aloud. In every home in Egypt the same sad cry arose, "Our eldest child is dead!" What a bitter time!

Not waiting until morning should come, Pharaoh sent a swift messenger to Goshen in search of Moses and Aaron. There he found everyone wide awake, all of them ready to start on their journey. "Pharaoh has sent word that you and all your people must leave Goshen at once," the messenger said. "And he demands that you take everything with you just as you have requested. Do not leave anything behind." The Egyptians, too, sent messengers to Goshen and urged the Israelites to hurry out of the land. "We shall all die if you stay here longer," they said.

For many years the Israelites had been slaves. They had no money and they had nothing that could be used as money. Now, at God's command, Moses told the people to ask their Egyptian neighbors for jewels of silver and of gold. And the Egyptians opened their treasure-boxes and gave freely to the Israelites. So eager were they for the Israelites to go away that they were willing to give them anything for which they asked.

And very early in the morning, without waiting to eat breakfast, the Israelites began to leave Goshen. Like a great army, six hundred thousand men with their wives and children marched out of Egypt. They took also their flocks of sheep and herds of cattle. The women had mixed dough in their pans for bread but had not put leaven, or yeast, in it to make it rise. They carried the pans on their heads, as people carry loads in that country. When they stopped to eat, they baked the dough in cakes over coals of fire, and this was called unleavened bread. And a rule was made that for one week in every year the Israelites should eat bread without leaven, or yeast, in it. This week was afterward celebrated as a feast, and was called the Feast of the Unleavened Bread.

Moses and Aaron led the people out of Egypt just as shepherds lead their sheep to fresh pasture-lands. But they did not choose the way to go; for God went with them, and he chose the way. In the daytime he concealed his presence in a great cloud, which moved slowly before the people, and at night, when they rested, he watched over them through a pillar of fire. By day or by night the Israelites could look upon the cloud or the pillar and say, "Our God is going with us, and he is leading the way."

Among the things that the Israelites carried out of Egypt was a coffin. In this coffin the body of Joseph had rested for hundreds of years. You remember that before Joseph died he commanded the Israelites not to bury him in Egypt, but to place his body in a coffin and carry it back to Canaan when they should return some day to live again in that land. He asked to be buried in the cave where Abraham, and Isaac, and Jacob, his father, had been buried. And now, though long years had passed, the men who were the great-great-grand-sons of this mighty prince in Egypt were now carrying his bones back to be buried in the land God had promised to his people.

Exod. 14:1–15:21

When the Israelites came into Goshen, they numbered only seventy people. Now when they were returning again to Canaan they numbered many thousands.

This great army was divided into twelve companies, or tribes, and these tribes were called after the names of Israel's sons. There was the tribe of Reuben, Israel's eldest son, in which every one was a descendant of Reuben; and the tribe of Simeon, Israel's second son, in which every one was a descendant of Simeon. And so it was in each of the twelve tribes, which bore the names of Israel's sons.

After this great company left Goshen, with their flocks and herds, God led them by the cloud to the shore of the Red Sea. Here they camped. Then they planned to rest from their march.

But suddenly a cry rose in the camp, "Pharaoh's army is coming upon us! We shall be taken as prisoners or else be killed!" The people looked, and sure enough, Pharaoh's army was coming behind them and shutting them away from the only road to safety. They could not swim across the sea. Neither could they fight against Pharaoh's skillful soldiers, for they had never been trained for battle. How frightened they were!

At first the people blamed Moses for bringing greater trouble upon them than they had ever known before. But Moses was not to blame. He had only followed the cloud in which God's presence dwelt, and the cloud had led them here. God wished to show his great power once more to the proud king who refused to obey him.

When Moses cried to God for help, the Lord told him to speak to the people and quiet them. They were all crying out in fear. He commanded them to stand still and see the wonderful path God was making for their escape. Then the cloud moved backward and stopped between their camp and Pharaoh's army. To the Israelites the cloud became a pillar of fire and lightened their camp all the night, but to the Egyptians the cloud became all darkness.

God told Moses to stretch his rod over the water of the Red Sea and divide it into two seas. Moses obeyed, and God sent a strong wind, which swept a wide path through the waters and dried the ground. On each side of this path the waters rose like a high wall, and stood still until every one of the Israelites and their flocks and herds had crossed in safety to the other side.

Now Pharaoh's heart had hardened again after he sent the Israelites out of Goshen. And Pharaoh said, "I have made a great mistake by letting all my slaves go free. I must send my army after them and bring them back." So he had followed the Israelites. When the cloud lifted and he and his army saw the Israelites walking through the sea upon a dry path between two walls of water, they rushed after them. For a while all went well, but when Pharaoh's army was far out from the shore, trouble came upon him and his soldiers. The horses became tangled in the harness and their feet began to sink in the sand. The chariot wheels came off. "Let us go back!" the soldiers cried. "Israel's God is fighting against us!" But it was too late; they could not go back, for the walls of water on each side fell down and the whole army was drowned.

This was a great deliverance to the Israelites. They saw that God had saved them from their enemies, and that he had even destroyed the ones who troubled them so many years. Now they were free from slavery.

Moses wrote a beautiful song about this deliverance, and all the people sang and rejoiced together. The women played musical instruments called timbrels, and followed Miriam, the sister of Moses and Aaron, through the camp, singing praises to God.

Exod. 15:22–27

After the Israelites celebrated their great deliverance from the Egyptian army, they began their march across the Wilderness of Shur. This was a country very unlike the land of Goshen. No waving fields of grain could they see, no grassy pasture-lands could they find for their flocks and herds. On every side the country looked barren and dreary. By and by they came to a camping place called Marah, and here they found more trouble.

The Israelites began to learn that trouble came in other countries besides Egypt, and from other causes besides wicked taskmasters and proud, hard-hearted, selfish kings. In this wilderness they were suffering because they could find no water to drink. The cattle and sheep were thirsty, too, and everyone was tired from the long march across the barren country. At Marah they found a spring of water, and with a glad cry they ran forward to get a drink. But the water was so bitter they could not swallow it. How unhappy they felt! They looked unkindly at Moses and were ready to blame him again for their troubles.

Moses, too, was thirsty, and he felt sorry for the people. But instead of growing impatient and ugly, he cried to God for help. And God told him what to do.

Near the spring where the bitter water was found grew a tree. God told Moses to cut this tree down and throw it into the spring. Moses did so, and the waters became sweet. Then the people drank deeply and were satisfied. The cattle and sheep, too, had an abundance to drink.

God wished to teach the people to trust him as their helper when troubles came. He probably wished to show them by this miracle how he could heal their bodies when sickness should come upon them. He also promised that if the people would obey his voice and do right, he would not let them suffer from any of the diseases that he had sent upon the Egyptians.

From the camp at Marah the Israelites moved forward again, and came to another stopping place. Here they found a beautiful grove of palm trees and twelve wells of water. The name of this place was Elim. The people pitched their tents beneath the trees and drank from the wells. They were glad to find such a pleasant place to camp in the wilderness.

The Israelites enjoyed their rest at Elim; but after some days the cloud in which God's presence dwelt lifted and began to move slowly away. By this sign the people understood that God wished to lead them farther on their journey. So they took down their tents and prepared to start forward again.

Now they entered a great desert country that lay between Elim and the mountain where God spoke to Moses from the burning bush. This country was called the Wilderness of Sin.

Like fretful children, the Israelites began to find fault with Moses and Aaron. First one thing, then another, displeased them. They could find so little food to eat in the great wilderness, and they grew hungry. Then they forgot how much they had suffered in Egypt. They forgot how many times God had helped them out of trouble. They thought only of their hunger, and of their unhappy state. They said, "We wish we had never left Egypt, for there we always had plenty to eat. We would rather have died there than die in this dreary country."

Moses heard the people complain and he was grieved. God, too, heard them. He spoke to Moses and said, "The people are sinning against me when they find fault with you because you led them out of Egypt. I shall not let them die of hunger, but I have brought them to this place so that they may know that I am the giver of all their blessings. In the evening I shall send meat to them, and in the morning I shall give them bread from heaven."

Then Moses called the people together to hear the words of the Lord. While Aaron spoke to them they looked toward the wilderness and saw in the cloud a glorious light. They knew God had heard their complaints.

In the evening a great many quails flew into the camp, and the people killed them for meat. The next morning a heavy dew lay on the ground. When the sun beamed down warm and bright the dew disappeared, and left the ground covered with something which looked white, like frost. "What is this?" the people asked each other when they looked out of their tents and saw the strange food lying on the ground. In their language "what is this?" are the words "man hu," and so the people said to each other, "Man hu? Man hu?" Afterward the food was called manna.

Moses told the people that God had sent this food to be their bread. "Go and gather it," said he, "and bring as much as you will need for today. Do not keep any in your vessels for tomorrow, because God will send a fresh supply. Each morning he will cause this bread to fall, except on the morning of the seventh day. On the sixth day you must gather twice as much as usual, and what is left after you have eaten of that gathering you may keep for the seventh day. It will not spoil on the seventh day, because God wishes you to keep that day as a holy Sabbath and do no work."

At Moses' bidding the people rushed out with vessels and gathered the manna from the ground. They cooked it, and the taste of this food pleased them. They were glad God had supplied their need.

Now, some of the people were not careful to obey Moses. When they saw they had prepared more manna than was needful for one day they kept it until the next morning. But the bread was no longer fit to eat, and they had to go out again to gather a fresh supply. And some failed to gather twice as much as usual on the sixth morning. But when they went out with their vessels on the Sabbath morning to pick up the wonderful bread they could find none. God was not pleased because they had disobeyed. And they had nothing to eat on that Sabbath.

From this time God sent manna to the Israelites every morning, except on the Sabbath, until they came to the land of Canaan.

Exod. 17–18

L eaving the Wilderness of Sin, the Israelites came to a place called Rephidim, and here again the cloud stopped as a sign that they should camp and rest from their journey.

But the people began to complain at once. Although God was sending bread to them every day, now he had led them to a place where no water could be found —not even a spring of bitter water. And they were thirsty. Coming to Moses, they asked impatiently that he give them some water to drink. But Moses was as helpless as they. Everywhere he searched for water, but nowhere could he find a drop. The people grew more impatient and restless. Finally they cried, "Why did you bring us and our children and our cattle out to this dreadful place to kill us with thirst?" Instead of asking God to help them, they were complaining against Moses, and some were even ready to kill him.

Then Moses cried aloud to God for help. The Lord told him to call the chief men of each tribe and take them with him to Mount Horeb. There God told him to strike a certain rock with his rod, while the men stood nearby. Although no springs or rivers were in sight, when Moses struck the rock a stream of clear water flowed from it and ran down the mountainside into the valley where the people were camping. Here again God helped when they were in trouble.

In the country around Rephidim a wild people lived who were called Amalekites. These people attacked the Israelites, and tried to steal their goods.

Moses chose a brave young man named Joshua to lead the army of Israel against their enemies. And while they fought, Moses stood on a hilltop and watched the battle. Aaron and Hur stood by him. Moses stretched his arms toward heaven and prayed God to help his people. In his hand he held the rod with which so many miracles had been performed. And the men of Israel drove their enemies back into the wilderness. But the battle was not yet ended.

Finally Moses grew very tired, and his arms fell to his sides. Then the Amalekites turned about and drove the men of Israel back. Moses saw at once that God was not helping his people when he was not holding the rod aloft. So he lifted it toward heaven once more. When his arms grew very tired again Aaron and Hur brought a large stone for Moses to sit upon. Then they stood, one on each side of him, and held up his arms until evening. The battle then ended, and Joshua returned with his men to the camp at Rephidim. The people knew God had helped them to drive their enemies away.

At this place Moses built an altar, to worship God.

One day while the Israelites were camping at Rephidim some visitors from Midian came to see Moses. They were Jethro, Moses' father-in-law, and Zipporah, Moses' wife, and Gershom and Eliezer, Moses' sons. Jethro had heard how wonderfully God saved the Israelites from Pharaoh's slavery, and he wished to talk with Moses. He brought sacrifices to offer upon the altar that Moses had built, and the Israelites also worshiped with him before the Lord. During his visit Jethro told Moses how to judge the people and how to lessen his burden. Then he bade Moses good-bye and went to his own country.

Exod. 19–24

Mount Horeb was the place where God had talked to Moses from a burning bush. This mountain was also called Sinai. In front of this mountain lay a wilderness, which was also called Sinai. When Moses tended sheep for his father-in-law he used to lead the flocks through this wilderness. He learned where to find grassy plains and plenty of water. And now he brought the Israelites from Rephidim to this place, and they camped under the shadow of the great, rock-walled mountain.

While the people were busy arranging their tents and preparing food, Moses climbed the mountain to talk with God. And the Lord said, "Tell the people that I shall speak to them from this mountain. On the third day I shall speak, and they shall hear my voice. Go, now, and bid them wash their clothes and make ready to meet me."

When the Israelites heard Moses' words they grew busy at once. Every one found something to do. Some carried water from the springs, and others washed soiled clothing. They were getting ready for a special time, when they might stand with Moses before God.

On the third morning a thick, dark cloud rested on top of Mount Sinai. Terrible thunders rolled down the mountainsides into the valley, and sharp lightnings broke through the thick cloud and flashed across the sky. The whole mountain shook. The Israelites had never seen nor heard such before, and now they trembled in their tents.

Then a trumpet sounded from the mountaintop. Perhaps an angel blew it. God had told Moses to gather the people together when they should hear the sound of a trumpet. And now they gathered together near the foot of the shaking mountain and listened to hear God's voice. Moses said, "Do not come any nearer, for God has said the mountain is holy and that if you touch it you shall die."

The trumpet sounded louder, and the mountain began to smoke as though a great fire were burning on the inside. Then Moses called, and a voice answered him from the mountaintop. It was the voice of God. And this voice spoke the words of the Ten Commandments so that all the people heard. As they listened great fear came into their hearts. They hurried back into the valley. And they cried to Moses, "Let not God speak to us in this voice of thunder, for we shall die. We will hear when you speak his words, and we will obey them."

Moses answered, "Do not be afraid when God speaks. He wishes to teach you that he is a great God, and holy. He wants you to serve him only, and never to bow down to other gods, as other people do."

Still the people stood far off, for they were afraid. But Moses was not afraid. He went into the thick darkness where God was, and listened while God told him about the many laws that he wanted the Israelites to obey. And Moses wrote the words of God in a book.

When Moses came down from the mountain, he told the people all the words God had spoken; and they answered, "We will be obedient."

Early in the morning of the next day, Moses built an altar under the shadow of the great mountain, and the young men brought offerings of oxen to give to the Lord. The people assembled again, and Moses read to them from the book of the covenant. Then they said, "All that God has spoken we will do. We will be obedient." And Moses took blood from the offerings of oxen, which the young men had brought, and sprinkled the blood upon the altar and upon the people. He said, "This is the blood of the covenant." We remember that a covenant made by God is a promise that will never be broken if the people to whom the promise is made will be obedient.

When this solemn service ended, the people went back to their tents in the valley, and Moses took Aaron and his two sons, Nadab and Abihu, and seventy of the old men with him up the mountain. God had commanded them to worship him there. And they saw the glory of God and they were not afraid. But they did not come near to the wonderful brightness of His glory. Only Moses came near.

After this time Moses went up on the mountain again, and took Joshua with him. He commanded the people to be obedient to Aaron and Hur until he should return. For forty days he listened to God's words, and the Lord gave him two flat tablets of stone upon which he had written with his own hand the words of the Ten Commandments. These were the words he spoke in a voice of thunder to the people.

THE TEN COMMANDMENTS

THOU SHALT HAVE NO OTHER GODS BEFORE ME.

THOU SHALT NOT MAKE UNTO THEE ANY GRAVEN IMAGE, OR ANY LIKENESS OF ANYTHING THAT IS IN HEAVEN ABOVE, OR THAT IS IN THE EARTH BENEATH, OR THAT IS IN THE WATER UNDER THE EARTH: THOU SHALT NOT BOW DOWN THYSELF TO THEM, NOR SERVE THEM: FOR I THE LORD THY GOD AM A JEALOUS GOD, VISITING THE INIQUITY OF THE FATHERS UPON THE CHILDREN UNTO THE THIRD AND FOURTH GENERATION OF THEM THAT HATE ME; AND SHOWING MERCY UNTO THOUSANDS OF THEM THAT LOVE ME AND KEEP MY COMMANDMENTS.

THOU SHALT NOT TAKE THE NAME OF THE LORD THY GOD IN VAIN; FOR THE LORD WILL NOT HOLD HIM GUILTLESS THAT TAKETH HIS NAME IN VAIN.

REMEMBER THE SABBATH DAY TO KEEP IT HOLY. SIX DAYS SHALT THOU LABOR, AND DO ALL THY WORK; BUT THE SEVENTH DAY IS THE SABBATH OF THE LORD THY GOD: IN IT THOU SHALT NOT DO ANY WORK, THOU, NOR THY SON, NOR THY DAUGHTER, NOR THY MAN SERVANT, NOR THY MAID SERVANT, NOR THY CATTLE, NOR THY

STRANGER THAT IS WITHIN THY GATES: FOR IN SIX DAYS THE LORD MADE HEAVEN AND EARTH, THE SEA, AND ALL THAT IN THEM IS, AND RESTED THE SEVENTH DAY: WHEREFORE THE LORD BLESSED THE SABBATH DAY, AND HALLOWED IT.

HONOR THY FATHER AND THY MOTHER: THAT THY DAYS MAY BE LONG UPON THE LAND WHICH THE LORD THY GOD GIVETH THEE.

THOU SHALT NOT KILL.

THOU SHALT NOT COMMIT ADULTERY.

THOU SHALT NOT STEAL.

THOU SHALT NOT BEAR FALSE WITNESS AGAINST THY NEIGHBOR.

THOU SHALT NOT COVET THY NEIGHBOR'S HOUSE. THOU SHALT NOT COVET THY NEIGHBOR'S WIFE, NOR HIS MAN SERVANT, NOR HIS MAID SERVANT, NOR HIS OX, NOR HIS DONKEY, NOR ANYTHING THAT IS THY NEIGHBOR'S.

While Moses was up on top of Mount Sinai talking with God, and Joshua was waiting for him on the mountainside, the Israelites could see from their tent doors in the valley what seemed to be a flame of fire leaping up toward the sky, day and night, from the place where Moses was in the thick cloud. They knew this was a sign of God's presence on the mountain.

But when the days passed by into weeks and still Moses did not return, the Israelites began to think he would never come back to them again. They grew restless. They soon forgot the great terror that filled their hearts when God's voice thundered to them from the smoking mountain in words they understood. They seemed to forget even the words that God spoke. And then it was easy to act as though they had forgotten their promise to Moses, that they would obey the words of the Lord.

One day they came to Aaron and said, "We know something dreadful has happened to Moses, because he does not come back." They complained because Moses had led them into the lonely wilderness and left them without a brave leader to take his place. Every day they grew more restless. Finally they planned to go on without Moses. So they came to Aaron and said, "Make us gods to go before us and show us the way."

Now Aaron was not a brave man. He feared the people. He remembered the time when they wanted to kill Moses because they could find no water, at Rephidim. Perhaps he thought they would throw stones at him and kill him if he refused to do as they asked. So he did not point them to the flame of fire that still leaped toward the sky from the mountaintop, where God was talking with Moses. He did not remind them of their promise to serve no other God except the One who spoke to them in a voice of thunder. Instead of bravely doing these things, he told them to bring their golden earrings, which the Egyptians had given them before they left Goshen. Then he took the gold that they brought and melted it carefully in a fire. When it was melted together, he shaped the mass of gold into the form of a calf, or a young ox, such as the Egyptians worshiped. This calf he set up in the middle of the camp.

Then the Israelites made a great feast and began to worship the golden calf, just as they had seen their Egyptian neighbors worship oxen at their temples. This was very wicked. As they bowed themselves before the idol and sang and danced around it they broke two of the Ten Commandments which God had given them to obey. In the first commandment God had said, "Thou shalt serve no other gods"; and in the second commandment he had forbidden them to worship before anything they made, calling it a god. Now they were even crying out, "This is the god that brought us out of Egypt!"

And God saw the golden calf. He saw the Israelites bowing down and worshiping it. He heard them singing and dancing around it. And he was greatly displeased. He said to Moses, "The Israelites have sinned against me. They have broken their promise and made a god of gold. Now they are worshiping it, and crying, 'This is the god that led us out of

Egypt!' Let me alone, Moses, and I will quickly destroy them all, for they are not fit to be called my people." God promised to raise up another nation from the children of Moses to be his chosen people.

But Moses loved the Israelites even though they had sometimes been unkind to him. He did not want God to destroy them all. So he prayed earnestly for God to spare their lives even though they had sinned greatly. He believed they might yet learn to serve the true God. And because Moses prayed for them, the Lord did not destroy them as he had planned.

Then Moses hurried down the mountainside with Joshua, carrying in his arms the two wonderful tablets of stone upon which God had written the words of the Ten Commandments. It was hard for Moses to believe the Israelites had sinned so greatly. But as they came nearer the valley Joshua said, "I hear the sound of war in the camp." Then they saw the people dancing and shouting before the god Aaron made.

Moses understood now why God wished to destroy the Israelites. The sight of their idol-worship filled him with great anger. He threw the wonderful tablets of stone upon the rocks at the foot of the mountain path and broke them in pieces. Perhaps he thought, "What is the use of keeping these tablets when the people have already broken two of the great commandments God wrote upon them?" Then he rushed into the camp and tore the idol down before the people. He broke it in pieces and threw it into the fire, he ground it into fine dust and threw the dust into the water from which the people drank. This made the water taste very bitter indeed, but Moses compelled the people to drink it.

Moses' sudden appearance in the camp broke up the merry feast. His anger quieted the people. But many of them were sorry he had come back. They wished to keep on worshiping the god Aaron had made. Then Moses called Aaron and asked, "What have these people done that you have brought this terrible sin upon them?"

And Aaron answered, "Do not be angry with me! You know these people, how their hearts are evil. And when they asked me to make a god for them to worship I told them to bring their golden earrings. I cast the earrings into the fire, and this calf came out!"

Moses was still angry. He cried to the people in a loud voice, "Whoever is on the Lord's side, let him come and stand by me!" Then every man who belonged to the tribe of Levi left the Israelite host and stood by Moses. Then Moses told these brave men to take their swords and go through the camp and kill every person they found who still wanted to worship the golden calf. "Do not spare one of them," he commanded. And the men killed three thousand people that day.

This was a sad time in Israel's camp. But no one was quite so sad as Moses. He understood how terrible was the sin of his people and he feared that God might never forgive them. The next day he called them together and said, "You have done very wickedly, and in God's sight your sin is very great. I will go up to him now and will make an offering for your sin. Perhaps he will forgive you."

And Moses went before the Lord and offered himself to die with the people. But God said, "Those who have sinned against me must suffer for their own sins."

Then God told Moses to cut two tablets out of stone like the ones he had broken, and bring them up on the Mount. And God wrote on those tablets the same words as he had written upon the others, and God talked with Moses again for forty days and forty nights on top of the mountain.

Exod. 34–39; Numbers 1–5

The Israelites were glad when they heard that Moses was coming down from Mount Sinai with two stone tablets in his arms the second time. They went out to meet him. Although he had been gone forty days and nights, this time they had not complained, nor wished to worship another god. But when they saw him coming they were afraid. They all turned back toward the camp.

Moses could not understand why they should be so frightened. He called to them, and the rulers of the people stopped. Then they turned around and went back again with Aaron to meet Moses. They told him why everyone was afraid of him. They said, "The skin of your face is shining with a strange light, like the sun, and we cannot look upon it." Moses did not know that God's glory was shining upon his face. But he put a veil over his face, and then all the Israelites came back and listened to his words.

God had given to Moses the rules that he wished the people to obey. These rules, or commandments, Moses wrote in a book. But the Ten Commandments, which God had spoken to the people in a voice of thunder, God himself wrote upon the two tablets of stone. Whenever Moses told the people about God's words he wore a veil over his face, but whenever he talked with God he took the veil off.

Now the time had come when God wanted to let the people know that he was living among them, right in their camp. He wanted them to have a certain place where they might always worship him. He wanted them to build such a place, where the sign of his presence might dwell just as it dwelt in the cloud by day and the pillar of fire by night.

The Egyptians had temples built of stone, where they worshiped their gods. They had idols of gold and idols of silver and living animals in their temples, before which they bowed down and worshiped. This kind of worship is called idolatry.

God wanted the Israelites to be his own people. He wanted them to act differently from other people. He wanted them to worship him only, because he is the only true God. So he told Moses about his plan to dwell among the people, and he showed Moses how to build the place of worship.

When the people heard about God's plan to live among them, they were glad. They offered cheerfully to give the best of everything they had to help build a place where they might worship the Lord, their God. They brought gifts of gold and of silver, of jewels, of wood, and of beautiful linen cloth. They brought also the skins of animals. And God chose two wise men, named Bezaleel and Aholiab, to teach other men how to use these gifts and make everything for the place of worship.

Now the people themselves were living in tents. These dwelling places they could easily move about from one camp to another as they journeyed toward Canaan. God told Moses to build the place of worship somewhat like a tent, with board walls and with the top of cloth and animal skins, so that it could be taken apart and moved easily when the people moved their camp. This kind of place was called a tabernacle.

And God told the people exactly what kind of material he wanted them to use when they made the tabernacle. He told them what kind of furniture he wanted them to put inside the tabernacle. And he told them how to make the furniture and where to place each piece of it.

The people were careful to obey all the words of the Lord. They worked faithfully and brought more gifts than were needed for the building.

When everything was finished, God told Moses to set up the tabernacle in the middle of the camp. And he chose the men of the tribe of Levi to take care of the tabernacle. Moses and Aaron belonged to this tribe. God told Moses to divide the whole tribe of Levi into three groups, one group for each of Levi's sons. And God said these three groups should camp one on the north side and one on the south side and one on the west side of the tabernacle. Moses and Aaron set their tent-homes on the east side, or in front of the door of the tabernacle.

After this time, when God chose men from the twelve tribes to go out to battle against their enemies he did not take any men from the tribe of Levi. He divided the tribe of Joseph's descendants into two separate tribes, and these tribes were given the names of Joseph's two sons, Ephraim and Manasseh. In this way he still had twelve tribes to go out to battle, and twelve tribes to camp, three on each of the four sides, around the place of worship.

The tabernacle, where the Israelites worshiped God, was surrounded by an uncovered space, called a court. This court was closed in by curtains, which were made of fine linen, and hung upon brass posts. The curtains were between seven and eight feet high. At the end toward the east was an opening, through which the priests and their helpers might enter.

Near the entrance, or door of the court, stood a great altar. This was called the "altar of burnt offering." You remember that whenever people of those times wished to worship God they built altars. Upon those altars they laid their gifts and sacrifices and burned them. They always built their altars of earth or of stones piled up. This altar of the tabernacle was built differently. It was built of thin boards, because God wanted the people to carry it with them wherever they journeyed. It was like a square box without a bottom or top, and covered on the inside and on the outside with brass so that it would not catch fire and be burned. Inside this altar a metal grating was fastened on which the fire was kindled. The ashes would fall through this grating to the ground. The altar was about five feet high and about seven feet square. Two long poles were fastened to two opposite sides of it, through rings at the corners, and whenever the Israelites moved their camp the priests carried the altar by placing the poles upon their shoulders.

Near the altar of burnt offering stood a large basin, or tank, called a laver. When the tabernacle was set up, this laver was filled with water, to be used by the priests for washing their hands and feet, and perhaps for washing parts of the offerings. Much water was needed for the worship of the tabernacle.

Farther in the court stood the tabernacle itself. The walls of this place were made of boards covered with gold and placed on silver bases. The roof was made of four curtains, one laid above another. The inner curtain was of very beautiful cloth, while the outer curtains were made of skins of animals, to keep out the rain. The front of the tabernacle opened into the court. There was no door, but sometimes a curtain hung before the opening.

The tabernacle was divided into two rooms by a beautiful linen curtain, which hung from the roof. The first room, which opened into the court, was called the "holy place"; and the second room, which had no entrance except through the holy place, was called the "holy of holies."

In the first room were three things: a table, a golden candlestick, and a small altar. The table was covered with gold, and twelve loaves of bread were placed upon it, as if the people of each tribe were giving an offering of food to God. The golden candlestick was made of pure gold, and it held seven burning lights. The small altar was called the "altar of incense," because sweet perfumes were burnt upon it. The fire upon this altar was to be lighted from the altar of burnt offering. Everything in this room was made of gold or was covered with gold—even the board walls on each side. And the curtains and the ceiling were decorated with beautiful colors.

The second room contained only the "ark of the covenant." This ark was a box, or chest, covered entirely with gold, on the inside and on the outside. The lid of this box was called the "mercy-seat." At each end of the mercy-seat was a strange figure. These were called cherubim. They were made of gold. The two stone tablets upon which God had written the words of the Ten Commandments were placed within the ark of the covenant.

All the furniture of the tabernacle was built so that it could be easily carried from one place to another. And the board walls were made so that they could be taken apart and moved with the furniture and the brass posts and the curtains.

When the tabernacle was set up in the middle of the camp, God moved the cloud above it and filled it with his glory. Every day the cloud rested upon the tabernacle, and every night a flame of fire leaped from its roof. And all the people saw these things, and they knew that God was living among them.

Leviticus 1–10: 7

After the tabernacle was set up, Moses did not need to climb Mount Sinai any more to talk with God. Now he could enter the tabernacle, where God lived among the people, and hear the words of the Lord.

Before this time, whenever anyone wished to worship God, that one would build an altar and burn his offering upon it, calling on the Lord to forgive his sins. And the Lord would hear him. But now Moses told the people that whenever they wished to worship God and pray for the forgiveness of their sins they should bring their sacrifice to the men at the door of the court, whose duty it should be to tend the altar of burnt offering. Those men, Moses said, would be called priests. And the priests would offer the sacrifices of the people before the Lord, and God would accept them.

God chose Aaron to be the high priest, and to him he gave the most important work in the tabernacle worship. Aaron's sons God chose to be priests also, and they were to be Aaron's helpers.

On the morning when the tabernacle worship first began, God told Moses to call the people together before the door of the tabernacle, and there, in the presence of them all, to anoint both Aaron and his sons with oil and to put on them the beautiful priestly robes that they should wear. God wanted the people to see that he had chosen these men to do his work in the court, and in the tabernacle where no one else except Moses was allowed to enter.

After Aaron was made high priest he offered a lamb on the altar of burnt offering as a sacrifice for the sins of the people. He did not put any fire on the altar, but God sent fire, which burned up the lamb. When the people saw this they shouted with joy and fell down on their faces, because now they knew God was pleased with their offering and with their priests. From that time the priests offered two sacrifices for sin upon the altar of burnt offering every day — in the morning and in the evening. God reminded the people by these sacrifices that sin is an awful thing.

And the fire that God sent on the great altar was never allowed to die out. Every morning at sunrise the priests raked the coals and placed fresh wood upon them, to keep the fire burning brightly. Even when the tabernacle was moved to another camping place on their journey to Canaan, the priests would carry burning coals from the altar in a covered pan. God had lighted this fire, and they wished to keep it always burning.

Inside the holy place, you remember, was a second altar, called the altar of incense, upon which sweet perfumes were burned before the Lord. It was the duty of the priests every morning and every evening to carry a fire-shovelful of burning coals from the great altar to light the fire on the altar of incense. They carried these coals in a bowl that hung on chains. Such a bowl was called a censer. God commanded that the altar of incense should never be lighted by any other fire except from the one that he had kindled upon the great altar.

Another duty of the priests' was to keep twelve loaves of bread upon the golden table in the holy place. Each Sabbath morning they were to bring fresh loaves and remove the stale ones. These loaves were called shewbread. No one except a priest was permitted to eat this bread.

The priests also tended the seven lamps that burned on the golden candlestick. Every day they filled the lamp bowls with fresh oil, and they kept the lights always burning.

One day not long after the tabernacle worship had begun, a sad thing happened. Two of Aaron's sons, Nadab and Abihu, were preparing to light the fire on the altar of incense. They disobeyed God, and did not carry burning coals from the great altar but took other fire. And while they stood before the altar of incense in the holy place, suddenly they fell down dead. Thus God punished them because they had dared to disobey his word.

Moses would not allow Aaron nor his other sons to

touch the bodies of Nadab and Abihu. He called two men who were Levites, and cousins of the dead men, to carry the bodies away and bury them in the desert sand outside the camp.

This was a great lesson to Aaron and to his other sons. They saw that God expected them carefully to obey all of his words.

Num. 9–12

One day while the Israelites were still camping near Mount Sinai, God reminded Moses that a whole year had passed since they left Egypt. And God said, "The time has come when you must eat another Passover supper, for I want you to remember how the death-angel passed over your homes in Goshen." Moses told the people the words of the Lord; then every family in every tribe prepared a supper like the one they had eaten before Pharaoh drove them out of his country.

Not many days after this Passover supper had been eaten, the Israelites saw the cloud lift from above the tabernacle and float slowly away toward the north. They knew the time had come when they must journey on. They had lived for nearly a year in the wilderness of Sinai, under the shadow of the great mountain, and no doubt they felt glad to start forward again toward Canaan. They followed the floating cloud on and on across the barren country for the three days' journey. Then the cloud stopped, and while they rested in their tents some began to complain. God was much displeased at this, and he sent a fire among them. Many of those who complained were killed by the fire. The other people were frightened, and they cried to Moses for help. They thought they might all be killed. Then Moses prayed, and God took the fire away. Moses called the name of this camping place Taberah, which means, "A burning."

From Taberah the cloud led the Israelites farther north and brought them to the second stopping place. Here the people rested again. And here they seemed to forget the terrible punishment that had come upon those who complained at Taberah. They seemed to forget every blessing that God had sent to them. They said, "We are hungry for meat—oh, so hungry!" And they frowned when they saw the manna lying on the ground about their camp. "We are tired of this manna," they cried, "we want meat!" They talked to each other about the fish that they had eaten while they lived in Egypt, and about the vegetables that had grown in their gardens in Goshen. And the more they talked about these things the hungrier they became. Then instead of cheerfully gathering the fresh manna, which God sent every morning, and thankfully preparing it for food, they complained while they worked and they grumbled while they ate. Finally, like pouting children, they stood in their tent doors and wept because they had no meat.

Moses was very unhappy when he saw how foolishly the Israelites were behaving. Time after time they had complained, and just as often he had prayed for them. Now he did not want to pray for them. He told the Lord he was tired of leading such unthankful people. He even wanted to die. Poor, discouraged Moses!

God, too, was much displeased with the Israelites. He

knew they were unthankful and wicked. He knew they needed to be punished again. He felt sorry for Moses because the work was too heavy for him. He told Moses to choose seventy other men to help him in his work. And God caused those men to hear His words and to speak them to the people.

Because the people desired meat, God sent them birds, like quails. These he caused to come in great numbers outside the camp. When the people heard about them they rushed into the desert to gather the birds. For two days and one night they worked steadily, for God had sent enough meat to last them through one whole month. But they did not take time to thank God for his food. They thought only of satisfying their hunger. And thus they added more unthankfulness to their sins, and God punished them severely. While they were eating the meat God sent a sickness upon them and many died. And so here at this place, as at Taberah, they left behind them a graveyard where the dead bodies of their wicked relatives were buried. They called this place by the long name of Kib-roth-hat-ta-a-vah, which means, "The graves of lust."

When the cloud moved on, it stopped next at a place called Hazeroth. Here Miriam and Aaron, the sister and brother of Moses, found fault with Moses because he had married a woman who was not an Israelite. And they questioned why he should be the chief ruler among the people when God had sometimes spoken to them also. They allowed a wicked feeling of envy to grow in their hearts. They envied Moses because he was great in the eyes of all the people. They, too, wished to be rulers, and to be called great and wise. But God was angry with them, and he sent a dreadful disease, called leprosy, upon Miriam. Her skin became white like snow, and when Aaron saw what had happened he felt sorry because they had sinned against Moses and against God. He told Moses of his sorrow, and asked him to pray that Miriam might be healed. Moses was ready to forgive them both, and he prayed earnestly for Miriam. God heard his prayer, and after seven days Miriam was well again.

When the cloud lifted from Hazeroth, it did not stop again until the Israelites had entered the wilderness of Paran, which lies just outside of the promised land of Canaan.

Num. 13–14

The Israelites left the dreary desert behind them when they came to Kadesh-barnea, in the Wilderness of Paran. Now they were very near to Canaan, the land that God had promised to give them for their own country. Only one more march forward would take them across the border and into the beautiful country.

But the Israelites were not ready to enter Canaan. Although they had always taken down their tents and prepared to march whenever God showed by his signs in the cloud that they should go forward, now they said, "We do not know this country that lies before us. We are not ready to enter until we may know which way to go. Let us send men to pass through the land and search it. When they come again, they can tell us about what they have seen and which will be the safest road for us to travel." The people did not want to trust God to lead them into Canaan. Although he had done so much for them in the past, they seemed to distrust him now. He had marvelously delivered them from Pharaoh, king of Egypt. He had divided the Red Sea before them and brought them unharmed through its midst. He had brought them through the wilderness and protected them from the dangers of the way. He had overcome their enemies for them. He had saved their lives by giving them water out of the solid rock. He had even rained food upon them from heaven. Yet now they wanted to depend more upon themselves. And God let them have their own way.

God told Moses to choose twelve men, one man from each of the twelve tribes, and send them to search the land carefully. These twelve men were called spies, because they were sent to spy out the land of Canaan. Moses told them not to be afraid, for God would take care of them. And he commanded them to bring back some fruit from the land.

For forty days the spies went here and there through the promised land. They saw strong cities and small towns. They saw fields of grain and large vineyards with ripened grapes. They saw that the land was indeed beautiful, and that it was well supplied with foodstuffs. They knew that the Israelites would not need to grow hungry for meats and for vegetables in such a bountiful land.

At the end of forty days the spies returned to Israel's camp. They brought samples of the fruits that grew in Canaan. Two of them carried one large cluster of grapes on a staff between them. Never before had the Israelites seen such splendid fruit. Then ten of the spies began to tell about the land. "It is indeed a good country," they said, "but the people who live there are stronger than we. Many of them live in cities surrounded by great walls that seem to reach to the sky. Others of them are like giants—so powerful and so tall that we looked like grasshoppers in our own eyes. We were lucky to get back alive."

Those spies did not thank God for taking care of them. They did not believe God would help the Israelites to overcome the giants and to overthrow the walled cities. They had no faith in God. And when the Israelites heard their report they began to weep. Then Caleb, one of the spies who trusted in God, quieted them and said, "Do not be afraid, for we are strong enough to take the land. Let us go up at once, for we are well able to overcome it." But the people would not listen to his words. They began to weep aloud, and all through the night the noise of their weeping was heard in the camp. When morning came they began to complain against God. "We wish we had stayed in Egypt!" they said. "We had rather died back in the wilderness than to be killed by those dreadful giants in Canaan. Why has God brought us here to die? Our wives and our children will be taken for prisoners." Then they planned to choose a captain and return again to Egypt.

When Moses and Aaron heard about the plan they fell on their faces and begged the people to obey God. And Caleb and Joshua, the two spies who had faith in God, tore their clothes as a sign of deep sorrow and cried out to the people, "Do not sin so against the Lord! He has given us all the land before us, and he has taken away the courage of those who live in the land. We can easily drive them away. Let us go forward!"

Instead of listening to Caleb and Joshua, the people wanted to throw stones at them and kill them. But God would not allow them to harm his true men. While they were going about to do the evil deed, suddenly a bright light flashed upon them from the door of the tabernacle. And God spoke to Moses out of the light and said, "I am ready now to punish these wicked people with a terrible disease, which will kill them all. I am tired of their complaining and of their wicked plans. Although I have showed my great signs to them many times, still they will not trust me nor obey my words. I will take your children, Moses, and will make of them a great nation instead of the Israelites, and to them I will give the land of Canaan.

But Moses prayed earnestly for the people. He told the Lord that the Egyptians would hear about the death of the Israelites and they would say, "God was not able to bring them into Canaan, so he killed them in the wilderness." Moses reminded the Lord of his promise to be very merciful and to forgive wrong-doing.

And God for Moses' sake forgave the Israelites and did not destroy them completely. But because they had refused to go forward at the words of Caleb and Joshua, God said they should not be allowed to cross over into Canaan at that time. None of them from twenty years of age and upward should ever go into Canaan to live because they had said, "We had rather died in the wilderness!" To punish them God commanded that they should turn back again into the dreary wilderness and camp there until every man who had murmured should die. Then their children might go in and possess the promised land.

When the Israelites heard about this bitter punishment they did not want to go back. They said, "We will go forward, as the Lord first commanded us." And their men who had been trained for battle hurried out of the camp to fight against the men of Canaan. Moses called to them, "Don't go! God is not with you!" But they rushed on, paying no heed to Moses' warning, and the men of Canaan came out to meet them. The battle did not last long, for the Israelites had not obeyed God, and he would not help them. Soon the men of Canaan drove them out of their land, and the Israelites ran away from the battle into the wilderness.

Num. 16–17

One day a man named Korah began to think wrong thoughts about Moses and about Aaron. As time went on, he allowed those wrong thoughts to grow in his mind until they became very wicked. He told others about his thoughts, and soon many people were thinking wickedly, too.

Korah belonged to the tribe of Levi, to which tribe Moses and Aaron also belonged. God had chosen that tribe, you remember, to take care of the tabernacle. And he had chosen Aaron, one of that tribe, to be high priest, and Aaron's sons he had chosen to be priests. No other people except the high priest, the priests, and Moses were permitted to enter the tabernacle. And no other people except the

Levites were supposed to perform service at the tabernacle, because God had made the tabernacle a holy place and he had separated the Levites from the other tribes to take care of this holy place.

Korah thought, "I also am a Levite, and why am I not as good as Aaron?" And Korah envied Aaron. And two of Korah's friends, Dathan and Abiram, who belonged to the tribe of Reuben, heard Korah tell about his thoughts, and they said, "We are just as able to be rulers as is this man Moses." And they went with Korah and with two hundred and fifty other men who despised Moses and Aaron.

Finally all these men came to talk with Moses. They said, "You are lifting yourself above us as though you were some great person. We are just as good as you." They spoke also against Aaron, for they envied both of these men. And Moses was grieved to hear their words. He knew that he had not set himself up above them as some great person. He knew God had chosen him to be their leader and he was only obeying God. He knew, too, that God had chosen Aaron to be the high priest. These men were not really talking against Moses and Aaron, but against God.

Moses told Korah and the men who were with him to bring censers on the next day, with fire and with sweet incense in them, just as the priests brought censers before the Lord. He told Aaron to bring a censer also, and he said they should prove which man of them God had chosen to be their high priest.

Moses' words were told through all the camp, and on the next day the rest of the Israelites came with Korah and his friends. And Korah brought them all before the door of the tabernacle. And he took Dathan and Abiram and the two hundred and fifty men and stood in the door of the tabernacle, and every one of them placed a censer before the Lord, and Aaron, too, placed his censer before the Lord.

God was greatly displeased, and he told Moses to go quickly away from the people for he was going to destroy them at once. But Moses fell down on his face and cried to God to spare their lives. Because of this God said he would not destroy the Israelites if they would go away from Korah and his friends. When they heard this the people hurried away in every direction, leaving Korah and his friends alone by their tents. Then Moses said, "Now we shall prove whether I have ruled these people by God's command or whether I have chosen by myself to rule over them. If the ground opens up and swallows these men we shall know that God has called me to do this work." No sooner had Moses finished speaking than the ground opened up under the feet of Korah and his friends and they fell screaming into the depths of the earth. The Israelites fled in terror when they heard the screams of those who perished, for they thought the earth might swallow them up also.

We might suppose that the people surely would be afraid to speak against the Lord anymore, or against his true men. But on the very next day the Israelites began to say, "Moses and Aaron are to blame because Korah and all his friends were killed yesterday. Those were good people, too."

God heard their words, and he said to Moses and Aaron, "Go away from these people because I am ready to destroy them. They do not deserve to live." But Moses and Aaron fell down before the Lord again and prayed earnestly for the people. This time God would not hear their prayers. He sent a terrible sickness upon the people and they began to die everywhere in the camp. Moses was afraid they might all die. He told Aaron to take in a censer fire from the altar of burnt offering and burn sweet incense before God. And Aaron ran out among the people carrying the censer in his hand. He stood between those who had died and those who were yet alive. And God stopped the sickness that no more died of it.

Soon after this God commanded each of the twelve tribes to send Moses a rod. And he commanded Moses to write upon each rod the name of the tribe who had sent it. God said that Aaron's name should be written upon the rod of the tribe of Levi. Then God told Moses to place these twelve rods in the tabernacle before the ark and to leave them there until the next day. And God said, "The man whose rod shall grow is the man whom I choose to be my priest."

The next day Moses found eleven of the rods looking just the same as when he had placed them before the ark. But the one that had Aaron's name on it was blossoming like a growing branch upon a tree. Moses showed these rods to the people, and they knew by the sign of Aaron's blossoming rod that God had chosen him to be the high priest. God commanded Moses to keep Aaron's rod in the tabernacle so that the people might never forget to honor Aaron and his sons as God's chosen men for the priesthood.

Num. 20; Deuteronomy 2:1–15

For nearly forty years the Israelites went from one place to another in the great wilderness. They did not try again to enter Canaan, nor did they try to go back to Egypt. They waited for the time to come when God would be willing to lead them into the promised land.

During those long years of waiting only a few things happened that we may read about. Miriam, the sister of Moses and Aaron, died at Kadesh-barnea, and was buried there. About this time the wells at Kadesh dried up, and the people and their cattle and sheep could find no water to drink. They began to complain again, and God told Moses to take his rod and go with Aaron and all the people to a great rock not far from the camp. God said that Moses should speak to this rock in the presence of all the people. At Moses' word, God would cause water to flow out of the rock in a clear stream. From this all the people and all their animals might drink.

Moses and Aaron gathered the people together and went before them out to the great rock. Then, instead of speaking to the rock, as God had said they should, Moses spoke to the people in an angry tone and asked, "Must we bring water to you out of this rock?" Moses did not speak to the rock at all, but struck it with his rod. When no water came out he struck it again, and this time a clear stream gushed out and flowed across the sand. The people ran quickly to drink from it and to fill their vessels. The cattle and sheep also came to the stream and drank freely of the water God had sent.

God was not pleased with Moses and Aaron when they failed to do just as he had commanded them. Because of their disobedience, God said they should both die before the Israelites crossed over into the promised land.

Moses planned to lead the Israelites into Canaan from another point. To reach that point, he planned to go through the country of Edom, where the Edomites lived. These people were descendants of Esau, the brother of Israel (Jacob) from whom the Israelites had descended. Both the Edomites and the Israelites were descendants of Abraham and of Isaac, and Moses wished to be friendly with these people of such near kin. He sent a messenger to the king of Edom, asking him to let the Israelites pass through his country. "We will not enter your fields nor your vineyards," said the messenger, "and we will be careful to pay for the water that we drink from your wells."

But the king of Edom did not feel friendly toward the Israelites. He was afraid to let so many people pass through his country. He sent word back to Moses, saying, "You must not lead your people through Edom. If you try to pass through my land, I will fight against you with my army and will drive you back again into the wilderness."

Moses did not want to fight against a people who were so near of kin to the Israelites. He changed his plans and led the people around the country of Edom—south, and east, and north toward the eastern part of Canaan. On this long, tiresome journey across bare wildernesses and rocky plains, the Israelites passed Mount Hor.

While they were camping at Mount Hor, God told Moses to take Aaron and Eleazar, Aaron's son, up on the mountain, and to take off Aaron's priestly robes and put them on Eleazar. Aaron was now an old, old man, and the time had come when he must die. And God wanted Eleazar to become high priest after Aaron.

With a sad heart Moses climbed the rocky mountainside, taking his aged brother and his nephew along. And there he obeyed the words of the Lord, and there Aaron died. Then Moses returned to the camp again, with Eleazar, and all the people saw that Aaron did not come down with them. They saw, too, that Aaron's priestly robes were upon his son, and by this they understood that God had chosen Eleazar to be high priest in Aaron's place. They knew Aaron had died up on the mountain, and they mourned for him for thirty days.

Num. 21:4—9

After the Israelites left Mount Hor they came into a desert country where the hot sands burned their feet. Everything looked dreary, and Canaan seemed very far away. The people felt tired and unhappy. They began to complain again about their troubles. They said the manna no longer tasted good, and that they could find no water at all.

While they were complaining, God caused fiery serpents, or poisonous snakes that looked like fire and whose poison burned like fire, to crawl into their camp and bite many of the people. And those who were bitten died.

Now these Israelites were not so stubborn as their fathers had been, who forty years before this time had often sinned against God by complaining about their troubles. Nearly all of those old men had died. These younger men knew, when the fiery serpents came among them, that God was punishing them because they had sinned. And they were sorry for their wrong-doing. They came quickly to Moses and said, "We have sinned, for we have spoken against the Lord, and against you. We want you to pray for us, that God will take away these fiery serpents." Moses prayed, and God told him to make a serpent of brass, like a fiery serpent, and hang it on a pole and set the pole up in the middle of the camp. Then God commanded the people who were bitten by the snakes to look toward the serpent of brass, which Moses had set up. "Whoever looks toward that serpent," God said, "even though he is bitten by one of the poisonous snakes he shall not die." And the people who believed God's word and looked toward the serpent of brass were saved.

Num. 21:12–22:2

After the Israelites moved away from the camp where the fiery serpents had bitten them, they came to a wilderness near the land of Moah. Although they found no water in this wilderness, they did not murmur, because now they were willing to trust in God. And God told Moses to gather them together into one place and he would give them water.

When the people came together, Moses told the chief men of the tribes to dig a well in the sand. And while these men dug down to find springs all the people sang cheerful songs. They believed God would fill the well with good water even before they saw it bubble up from the deep springs. They pleased God by believing thus in him, and they enjoyed drinking from this wilderness well.

Nearby was the country where the Amorite people lived. These were wicked people, who worshiped idols. Because their country lay between the Israelites' camp and Canaan, Moses sent a message to Sihon, their king, asking him to let the Israelites pass through his land. But Sihon did not want them even to come near. He took his army and went out to fight against the Israelites. He thought he would drive them away, back into the wilderness.

But God helped the Israelites and gave them a great victory. They killed the wicked king and his soldiers, and afterward they marched into his country and took it for their own land. They drove out all the Amorites who were living in the villages, and they even went into the cities where Sihon and his soldiers had lived.

Soon after this the Israelites marched on into the land of Bashan. They did not even ask Og, the king of Bashan, to let them pass through his country. He, too, was a wicked king like Sihon had been, and his people also bowed down to worship idols. When Og heard that the Israelites were coming, he went out with his army to meet them and to fight against them. The Lord told Moses not to be afraid of this king nor of his army, for He would help the Israelites again. And when they fought, the Israelites killed the whole army of Bashan and took their country just as they had taken the land of the Amorites.

Now the long journey of forty years through the wilderness had come to an end. All of the old men except Moses and Caleb and Joshua had died in the wilderness. The Israelites had come again to the border of Canaan. Only the River Jordan separated them from the green hills and beautiful valleys of that promised land. They could look across the River and see the rich country, which God had promised to give to them for their own.

Num. 22: 1–35

While the Israelites were setting up their tents on the plains of Moab near the Jordan River, the king of that country was wondering what he should do to make himself and his people safe. He had heard what the Israelites did to Sihon, king of the Amorites, and he was afraid of them. He knew their army was larger than his. He knew they had taken the land of the Amorites and the land of Bashan for their own country. He thought, "They will take my country away from me, and they may even kill me."

Finally this king, whose name was Balak, decided to send for a wise man from Midian to come and help him. So he called some of his princes and sent them with this message: "A great host of people from Egypt have come into my country and they are too many for me to fight against. I want you to come and help me, for I have heard that you are very wise, and that whomever you speak against is made weak, and whomever you bless is made strong."

When the princes of Moab came to the wise man, whose name was Balaam, they delivered the messages of their king. And no doubt they showed Balaam the money that Balak had sent to pay him for his services. But Balaam said, "I do not know whether the Lord will let me go with you or not. Perhaps he does not want me to speak against the Israelites. Stay with me tonight, and in the morning I will tell whether I may go or not."

During the night God spoke to Balaam and asked, "Who are these men in your house?" And Balaam answered, "They are princes of Moab, who have come at their king's command to ask me to help him out of trouble. The Israelites, from Egypt, have come into his land with a strong army and he is afraid of them. He wants me to speak against them in your name, so that they will become weak." But God said, "You must not go to help the king of Moab. You must not speak against the Israelites; for I have blessed them."

When morning came Balaam told the princes that God would not let him go with them. And they hurried back to tell Balaam's words to the king.

But Balak sent the second time to Balaam. This time he sent other princes, who were greater than the first ones. He sent money also, and he promised to give great honor to Balaam if only he would come to help him.

Now Balaam wished to have the money that Balak sent. He wished also to receive the honor that this king promised to give him. As he thought about these things he wanted them more than ever. He knew God had said he should not go. But he decided to try once more, so he invited these princes to stay at his house until the next morning. And while they slept he heard God's voice again. This time God told him that if the men should waken him in the morning he might go with them. Only he should be careful to speak the words God would give him to speak.

Balaam was eager to go. He did not wait to see whether these princes would call for him in the morning, but rose early and saddled the donkey upon which he often rode. Then he took two of his servants and started out with the princes to see the king.

But God was displeased with Balaam. He sent his angel to trouble him, and the angel stood in the road and drew out his sword to kill Balaam. The donkey upon which Balaam was riding saw the angel and turned off from the road into a field. Balaam grew angry at this and struck her a blow. Back into the road they went, and presently they came to a place where a stone wall was built on each side. Here the angel stood again with his sword drawn, and here again the donkey saw the angel, while Balaam did not. The donkey was frightened again, and, trying to avoid the angel, she crowded closely against the wall on the opposite side. In doing this she crushed Balaam's foot against the wall. Now Balaam was quite angry, and he struck her a cruel blow.

Farther on the road they came to a very narrow place, and here the angel stood again. This time the donkey could not pass around, and, fearing the angel, she sank down on the ground beneath Balaam. At this Balaam's anger grew worse than ever and he struck a painful blow upon his faithful donkey with his staff. And God gave a voice to the donkey, and she spoke to Balaam. "What have I done that you should strike me these three times?" she asked.

Balaam was so angry he did not think it strange that a donkey could speak. He replied, "If I had a sword I would kill you, for you are not behaving as you should." Then the donkey asked Balaam whether she had not always carried him about safely since the day he bought her, and Balaam remembered that she had. And then God caused Balaam to see the angel standing before him.

Now Balaam was more frightened than the donkey had been. He fell down on his face before the angel. And the angel asked, "Why have you been beating your donkey? Three times she has seen me standing across your path and she has turned aside. Had she not done this I would surely have killed you, for I am much displeased with you."

Balaam cried, "I have sinned, for I did not know you were standing in the way to hinder me from going to see the king. Now I will turn back toward my home if you are displeased with my going on."

But the angel told Balaam to go on with the princes of Moab, and to be careful to speak only the words of the Lord.

Num. 22:36–32:9

When Balak heard that Balaam was finally coming he rushed out to meet him. He asked, "Why did you not come sooner?" and he told Balaam that he would give him a place of honor if only he would help in this time of trouble.

But Balaam answered, "I cannot promise to help you even though I have come. I can speak only the words that God gives me."

Perhaps Balak thought this wise man was trying to get more money from him by talking thus. He did not understand that Balaam could speak against people in the name of the Lord only when God wished to have him do this. Balak was an idol-worshiper, and he did not understand about the true God.

When Balaam saw all the money that Balak promised to give him he wished in his heart that he might please Balak and become a rich man. But he remembered the words of the angel, and he said, "I can speak only the words of the Lord."

Then the king took Balaam to the top of a mountain, from which they could look down upon the plain and see the Israelites' camp. And Balaam told the king to build seven altars on this mountain and offer to the Lord an ox and a sheep upon each of the altars. Balaam may have thought that God would be pleased with Balak's offerings and would then be willing to let him help Balak. But when Balaam went aside to hear God's words, he could hear only words of blessing for the Israelites. And he told these words to Balak, in the presence of the princes of Moab.

Now Balak was much displeased with Balaam because he had blessed the Israelites instead of speaking against them. He said, "Instead of helping me you are helping my enemies." But Balaam replied again that he could speak only the words that God gave him.

Balak thought he would try again. So he took Balaam to another place where they could see a part of the Israelites' camp. And here again he built seven altars and offered oxen and sheep to the Lord as he had done before. Still God would give only words of blessing to Balaam to speak about the Israelites.

When Balak tried the third time, and Balaam still failed to speak against Israel, the king became very angry. He thought that Balaam did not want to help him. He said, "I had planned to give you riches and honor, but your God has kept them from you. Now go in haste back to your own country. I am done with you because I see you are not my friend." And Balaam returned again to his home.

Although Balaam was careful to speak only the words of the Lord, yet down in his heart he wished he might please the king. Because he was a wise man he thought of another way to help Balak. Perhaps he thought Balak would still be willing to give him riches and honor. He told the king to act friendly toward the Israelites instead of trying to fight against them. And the king and all the people of Moab and of Midian, Balaam's country, were glad to do this.

But making friends with the Moabites and with the Midianites soon brought great trouble into Israel's camp. The young men of Israel began to marry these strange young women who worshiped other gods. And these young women took their husbands to the feasts of their gods and many of the Israelites bowed down to idols.

God saw the great danger of the Israelites becoming idolators, like the nations nearby, and forgetting him entirely. So he sent a plague into their camp, and many of these young people died. Then Moses took the men who were leading others into sin and caused them to be killed. After this the Israelites went to war against the Moabites and the Midianites and killed many of their people. And Balaam, the man who caused the Israelites to sin, was killed in his own land. He might have been a good man if he had always tried to please God; but because he loved riches and honor he disobeyed God.

Num. 27:12–23; Deut. 34

M oses was now an old, old man. His wonderful life had been divided into three parts. First he had lived as Pharaoh's grandson in the palaces of Egypt. Then he had worked as a shepherd in the wilderness. And the last part of his life he had spent among his own people, leading them from Egypt to the land that God promised to give them for their own.

And now, although Moses was very old, he still thought of the people—*his* people—and he asked God to set some other man before them to lead them after he should die. For God had told him that soon he must die, as Aaron had died, and as all the old men had died who came out of Egypt.

And God chose a man to take Moses' place. This man was Joshua, the one who had been with Moses on Mount Sinai and who had gone as one of the twelve spies from Kadesh into Canaan. Then, at God's bidding, Moses took Joshua and set him before the high priest, Eleazar, and laid his hands upon him and gave him some important work to do. By these acts the people understood that Joshua was soon to take up the work that Moses had done as their leader.

At this time the Israelites were living in the land that they had taken from their enemies. This land was good for pasture, and the Israelites kept many cattle and sheep. The men of Reuben's tribe and the men of Gad's tribe were all keepers of cattle. When they saw the rich pasture-lands of this country, they asked Moses to give them homes on this side of the Jordan River instead of giving them a part of the

land in Canaan. At first Moses did not want to do this; but
when the men promised to help the other Israelites fight
against their enemies in Canaan, Moses divided the land for
them. He gave a part of it to each of these tribes and a part
to half of the tribe of Manasseh.

After Moses had divided the country among these
tribes, he called the people together and told them again
about the words of command that God spoke to him on
Mount Sinai. He told them many things that they needed to
know before they should go into Canaan to live. He wrote all
these words in a book called Deuteronomy, which is the fifth
book in the Old Testament.

As the people listened to Moses' words they knew he
was soon going to leave them forever. They knew he had
been a faithful leader, and that he had loved them as dearly
as a father loves his own children. No doubt they felt sorry
because the time was soon coming when he could be with
them no more.

Then one day when Moses had ended his long farewell
talk with the people he walked away from his tent and away
out of the camp. All alone he went, and the people stood
watching him through their tears. They knew he was going
away to die. But first he was going to see the land of Canaan,
as God had promised him. Finally he came to Mount Nebo.
Up and up he climbed over the rocks, and higher he went
until the watchers on the plain could see him no more. Then
he looked from the top of that high mountain, and God
showed him the country where Abraham and where Isaac
had lived and died. What a beautiful country it was! As
Moses looked across its wooded hills and green valleys he

thought of the time soon to come when Joshua should lead the Israelites—*his* people—into that promised land.

Then God closed the eyes of this faithful old man, and folded his hands across his breast and carried his spirit away to a better land than Canaan. And God buried Moses somewhere in the plain, but no one knew where God had made the grave.

Thus ended the life of one of the greatest men this world has known, the only man who had ever talked face-to-face with God and whose face had shone with God's glory. And for thirty days the Israelites mourned and wept because their great leader had been taken away from them.

STORIES OF THE
NEW TESTAMENT

THE BIRTH OF JESUS

Luke 1:1–23

Zacharias, the priest, was an old man. All his lifetime he had been in the priesthood, for he was a descendant of Aaron. And he had married a woman named Elizabeth who also belonged to the family of the priests.

Zacharias and Elizabeth loved God and lived to please him as well as they knew how. They thought often of the promises God had given to the Jews by the old prophets who lived and died many years before their time. These promises were that some day God would send a Savior into the world, a son of David, to rule over his people forever.

Now Zacharias and his wife had grown old, and God had never given them any children. They had prayed many times and asked God to give them a little son or a little daughter, but their prayers had never been answered. And they had lived alone in their quiet home, thinking that God was not willing to bless them with the joy of parenthood. Still they served him faithfully, for they knew God always does what is best.

Zacharias did not always work in the temple. There were many priests, and these priests served in the temple by courses, just as David had planned when he arranged for the building of the first temple in Jerusalem. There were twenty-four courses of the priests, and Zacharias belonged to the course of Abia. When his turn came to serve he left his quiet home in the hill-country of Judah and went to Jerusalem. There he did the work that fell to him by lot. And his lot was to burn incense on the golden altar, in the holy place, or the first room of the temple, where only the priests might enter. Twice each day, at the time of the morning and the evening sacrifices, Zacharias took his censer of burning coals from the great altar and went into the holy place alone to offer sweet perfumes upon the golden altar before God. And while he lingered in that room, the people who came up to the temple to worship stood in the court outside and prayed. This was called the hour of prayer.

One day while Zacharias was offering incense upon the golden altar he was surprised to see an angel standing on the right side of the altar watching him. At first Zacharias was very much afraid, for he had never seen an angel before. But the angel said, "Do not be afraid, Zacharias, for your prayer is heard, and your wife shall have a son, whom you shall call John. This child shall bring you much joy, for he shall be great in the sight of the Lord. He shall never drink wine or strong drink, and he shall have God's Holy Spirit dwelling in him and giving him power such as Elijah had, to turn the people from their sins to serve God."

Zacharias listened, filled with wonder as to whether these words could be really true. He thought he and Elizabeth were too old to have a child, and he asked the angel to give him a sign that he might know for sure these things would happen. The angel answered, "I am Gabriel, the angel who stands in the presence of the Lord, and I have been sent by the Lord to tell you this glad news. But you have not believed my words, because you ask for a sign. Therefore this sign shall be given to you: You shall not be able to speak another word until the child is born." And then the angel disappeared as suddenly as he had come.

The people stood outside waiting and wondering why Zacharias was so long in the holy place. When he came out to them he could not speak, but showed them by motions that he had seen a vision from God.

Not long afterward Zacharias finished his course of service at the temple and returned to his home in the hill-country of Judah, as speechless as when he came out of the holy place. But he knew the time would come when his voice would return, for he believed the sign that the angel had given to him.

Matthew 1:18–25; Luke 1:26–56

Mary was a Jewish woman who had grown to womanhood in Nazareth, a city of Galilee. And she was expecting soon to marry a good man named Joseph.

Both Mary and Joseph were descendants of King David, but they were poor people. Joseph was a carpenter, and he worked with his tools to make a living for himself and to prepare a home for his bride.

One day God sent the angel Gabriel to Nazareth to speak to Mary, for God had chosen this young woman to become the mother of the Savior who would soon be born into the world.

Mary was surprised when she saw the angel, and she was more surprised when she heard his words. For he said, "You are highly favored and blessed among women, for the Lord is with you." Seeing that Mary did not understand his meaning, the angel told her that God was pleased with her and he had chosen her to become the mother of Jesus, the Savior of men. He told her that Jesus, her son, would be a King, and that he would rule forever. Even yet the surprised young woman could not understand his words, so the angel told her that this wonderful child would be called the Son of God.

While Mary listened the angel told her about the promised child of Zacharias and Elizabeth, the old people who lived in the hill-country of Judah. And he said, "Although they are old people, nothing is too hard for God to do." Then Mary knew that God could give her this wonderful child that the angel had promised, and she said, "Be it unto me according to thy word." So the angel left her and went back to heaven.

Now, Mary knew Elizabeth, the old lady of whom the angel spoke, for Elizabeth was her cousin. And she knew how Elizabeth had longed to have a child for many years.

She believed that her cousin must be very happy since God had promised to give her a child in her old age. Although the distance was great, she wished to see Elizabeth. So she decided to go and visit her.

As soon as Mary entered the home of her cousin and spoke words of greeting, God caused Elizabeth to know the secret that the angel had told this young woman in her own home. And Elizabeth rejoiced that Mary had come to visit her. She knew that Mary would some day be the mother of Jesus, the Savior of men.

The two women spent many happy days together, then Mary hurried back to her own home in Nazareth. There God's angel spoke to Joseph, the carpenter, in a dream, and told him about the wonderful secret of Jesus' birth. And Joseph was glad, for he had been longing for the time to come when the promised Savior should be born. He took Mary into his home and they waited for the angel's promise to come true.

Luke 1:57-80

A time of great rejoicing had come to the quiet little home in the hill-country of Judah, for God had sent the promised child to Zacharias and his aged wife, Elizabeth. And all the neighbors and relatives were rejoicing with these happy parents of the baby boy.

When the child was eight days old, preparations were made to give him a name, for this was the custom of the Jews. The friends and relatives said, "Let us call him Zacharias, after the name of his father."

But Elizabeth answered, "No, do not call him Zacharias, for his name is John."

"Why do you wish to call him John?" they asked in surprise. "You have no relatives who are called by that name." Then they turned to the old father, who had not spoken since the angel talked with him in the temple, and by making signs they asked him what they should call the child.

Zacharias understood what they wished to know, and he motioned for them to bring a writing table. This they did. Then he wrote in plain letters, so all could read, "His name is John."

"How strange!" thought the people. And all at once Zacharias began to speak to them again, just as he used to speak before he had seen the angel. And he praised God for giving him this wonderful baby boy.

News of this wonderful baby spread all through the hill-country, and people became much interested in him. They heard how the angel had appeared to Zacharias in the temple and promised that God would give the child, and they heard how Zacharias had been unable to speak from that time until after the baby was called by the name that the angel had given. They wondered much about these strange happenings, and they believed that surely the baby John would grow up into a great man.

Zacharias received wisdom from God and spoke words of prophecy to his neighbors and friends about his little son. He blessed the Lord. And then he said to his little boy, "You, my child, shall be called the prophet of the Highest, for you shall go before the face of the Lord to prepare his ways. You shall give knowledge of salvation to his people by the remission of their sins, through the tender mercy of our God."

Many other words did Zacharias speak; and his words came true, for the Spirit of God caused him to speak those words. And Zacharias cared for his little son as long as he lived. He watched with pride the changes that came with the years in the life of his little boy. And he saw that God was blessing John and causing him to grow strong and brave.

Perhaps Zacharias and Elizabeth did not live to see the day when John become a very useful man for God, for he did not begin his great work until he was thirty years old. Until that time he lived quietly in the desert country, and studied the books that God's prophets had written. He also listened much to the voice of God, and learned to understand God's will.

Luke 2:1–39

Out on the streets of Nazareth the people were standing in groups, talking excitedly. News had just reached their city that the great emperor of Rome had commanded all of them to go to the town or city from which their families had come and have their names written on lists. The emperor wished to have a list of the names of all the people in his great kingdom, or empire. And no one dared to disobey his command.

Soon travelers were seen going in every direction, for the emperor's command had been read in every city in the land. Out from Nazareth a company of people started toward the south, and in that company were Joseph and Mary, for they were both of the family of David, and they were going to

Bethlehem, the city of David, to have their names written upon the list at that place.

The road to the south led through the country of Samaria, then over the hills of Judah into Jerusalem. From Jerusalem Joseph and Mary went farther south, till they came to Bethlehem. Some of their company had left them in other cities along the way, while others had joined them. And when they reached Bethlehem they found that it was swarming with people who belonged, as they did, to the city where David was born. From every part of the land these people had come, and they had filled the lodging rooms till no more place could be found for the new arrivals.

The long journey from Nazareth had been very tiresome, and Mary longed for a place to rest. But Joseph could find no place except in the stable of the inn. And here they stayed during their first days in Bethlehem.

God had not forgotten his promise to Mary, and one night while she was in Bethlehem he gave her the child, Jesus. And Mary wrapped him in soft cloths called swaddling clothes, and laid him in a manger where the cattle fed, because she could find no better place.

The people of Bethlehem did not know that the angels were watching over the city that night. They did not hear the angels' glad song when Jesus was born. They did not see the joy of Mary and Joseph as they bent over the wonderful child in the manger. And so it was that God's greatest gift to men came right into that neighborhood and those people did not receive it as a gift from God because they did not expect a Savior to be born of such a humble person as Mary.

But there were shepherds watching their flocks that

night in a field near Bethlehem. Perhaps David, the shepherd king, had tended sheep in that same field many years before. These shepherds knew about David, and about God's promise to David that one of his descendants would be the Savior of men. And they may have been talking about God's promise when the angel of the Lord suddenly came near and a glorious light broke upon them through the darkness. Trembling with fear, they looked upon the angel and wondered why he had come to them. Then he spoke, and said: "Fear not, for I bring you good tidings of great joy, which shall be to all people. For unto you is born this day in the city of David a Savior, which is Christ the Lord. And you will find the baby wrapped in swaddling clothes and lying in a manger."

The shepherds listened eagerly to the angel's words, and when he finished speaking they saw a multitude of angels join him and begin to sing. Such music this world had never heard, for the angels were singing one of heaven's glad songs, giving glory to God in the highest. And they also sang, "Peace on earth, good will toward men."

When the song had ended, the angels went back into heaven and the glorious light faded again into the darkness of the still night. But the shepherds never forgot the sweetness of that song nor the joy it brought to their hearts. They did not wait until daylight to hasten to Bethlehem in search of the wonderful child, but said to each other just as soon as the angels disappeared, "Let us now go to Bethlehem and see this thing that the Lord has made known to us." So they left their flocks and hurried to Bethlehem, and there they found Mary and Joseph in the stable, with the infant Savior lying in the manger as the angel had said.

The shepherds told Mary and Joseph about their angel visitors and about the wonderful song that the angels sang. And no doubt they knelt before the manger and worshiped the little babe who lay quietly sleeping in the hay. Then they ran into the streets of Bethlehem and told every one whom they met about the angel's visit and about the wonderful child who had been born that night in a stable of the city. And the people wondered about the strange things that the shepherds told.

When the baby was eight days old, Joseph and Mary gave him a name, and they called him by the name the angel had chosen. That name, Jesus, means "salvation," and it told of the work that God had sent this child to do.

There was a law among the Jews that an offering should be made to the Lord for the first boy child born into each family. Among the rich people this offering should be a lamb, but among the poor people the offering of only two young pigeons would please God just as well. When Jesus was forty days old Joseph and Mary took him to the temple at Jerusalem to give their offering to the Lord. They brought two pigeons, for they were poor and could not bring a lamb.

An old man named Simeon was in the temple when Joseph and Mary came to bring their offering. This old man had served God for many years, and he longed to see the Savior whom God had promised to send into the world. God knew about this longing in Simeon's heart, and one day he spoke to Simeon and said, "You shall not die until you have seen the Savior."

When Mary brought the baby Jesus to the temple, God's

Spirit caused Simeon to know this child was the promised Savior. He came eagerly to meet Mary and took her babe in his arms. Then he said, "Now may God let me depart in peace, for I have seen with my eyes the salvation that he has sent."

Another faithful servant of the Lord was in the temple that day, an old lady named Anna, who spoke words of prophecy to the people. When she saw Jesus, she too gave thanks to God, and to the people who stood in the courts of the temple she spoke about this child of promise that had been sent from God to man.

Mary never forgot the words of these dear old people concerning her wonderful child. She remembered, too, the story that the shepherds had told, about the angels' visit to them, and about their words and song. Always in the days that followed Mary thought about these strange things and wondered how her son Jesus would finally become the King and Savior of the world.

Matt. 2

In the country far to the east of Judah there lived some wise men who studied the stars. One night they discovered a new star in the sky, one that they had never seen before. And God caused them to know by this star that Christ, the promised King of the Jews, had been born.

These wise men feared God, and they wished to see the child whom he had sent to be the Savior of the world. They supposed that the Jews must be very happy because God had at last sent to them the King he had promised.

Because these wise men were rich, they planned at once to make the long journey to Judah and bring precious gifts to the newborn King. Then they would worship him as their Savior.

For many days they traveled across the sandy desert, and at last they came to the fertile country where the Jews lived. They hurried on to the city of Jerusalem, for they expected to find the wonderful child living in the most beautiful place in all the land. And surely Jerusalem, the famous city of the Jews, would be the most beautiful place.

Herod, the man whom the emperor of Rome had set up over the land of Judah, was living in Jerusalem at that time. He was surprised when these strangers, riding on camels, came into his city and asked, "Where is the child that is born King of the Jews? We have seen his star in the far east country, and have come to worship him." Herod had heard nothing about this newborn King, and he was troubled. "What could this mean? he wondered. And even the rich people in Jerusalem were puzzled, too. They had heard nothing about Jesus.

No doubt the wise men were disappointed when they found that the rulers of Jerusalem knew nothing about the birth of the Savior. Perhaps they feared that they might have been mistaken, after all. But they waited anxiously while Herod called the chief priests and the scribes and asked them where the Savior should be born.

Now the chief priests and scribes were the men who read the books that the prophets had written long ago, and they understood that Christ should be born in Bethlehem. This they told to the excited Herod, and he called the wise men and told them that they should look for the child in Bethlehem.

Herod was troubled, because he did not want Jesus to become the King of the Jews. He thought this newborn King would take away his throne, and he wished to be king himself. But he did not let the wise men know about his troubled feelings. He called them and asked very politely when they had first seen this unusual star in the east, and they told him. Then he urged them to hurry on to Bethlehem and search diligently to find the child. "When you have found him," said Herod, "bring me word at once, that I, too, may go and worship him." And with these words he dismissed them from his presence.

The wise men mounted their camels again and took the south road, leading to Bethlehem. All day they had waited impatiently in Jerusalem, and now the shadows of night were falling over the land. But it would not be a very long ride to the birthplace of the newborn King, and, urged on by Herod's words, they hastened to find Jesus. Once outside the city gates, they saw the star, the same beautiful star that had shown so brightly in the east country, moving slowly before them, as if leading them on to the right place. Now they were sure that they had not been mistaken; and they rejoiced greatly, for they believed that God was in this manner trying to help them to find Jesus.

When they reached Bethlehem the star stood still over the place where Mary and Joseph were living. And the wise men knew they had followed the right guide, for here they found the wonderful child of whom the prophets had written. They knelt in humble worship before him, and then gave to him the rich treasures that they had brought from their homeland.

God spoke to the wise men in a dream one night while they were in Bethlehem, and warned them not to tell Herod that they had found Jesus. So they returned to their own country by another road, and Herod never saw them again. Not long afterward an angel of the Lord spoke to Joseph in a dream and said, "Arise, and take the young child and his mother, and flee into Egypt, and stay there until I bring word to you to return again, for Herod will seek for Jesus and try to destroy him."

Joseph rose up at once, and while it was yet dark he took Mary and the baby Jesus and hurried out of Bethlehem. For many days they traveled to the southwest, until they came to the land of Egypt. There they lived until an angel came to tell them that the wicked Herod was dead.

But Herod did not die for some time after the visit of the wise men. He waited long for them to return, bringing him word from Bethlehem as he had commanded them to do. But when many days passed and they did not come, he began to suspect that they had gone home without telling him of their wonderful discovery in Bethlehem. He believed they had guessed the reason why he had been so eager to see Jesus, and now he was angry because he had missed this opportunity to find the newborn King of the Jews.

Determined to destroy this King of the prophecies, Herod commanded his soldiers to go to Bethlehem and kill every baby there from two years old and younger. Not only to Bethlehem did he send them, but to the country places round about. And when this cruel deed was done he believed that he had surely gotten rid of this child whom the wise men sought to worship.

But all the while Jesus was living in safety among the people of Egypt, and fast growing out of his babyhood years. Then the wicked Herod died, and an angel came again to speak to Joseph, telling him to return with his wife and her child to their own land.

Joseph was glad to receive this message from the angel, for he loved to live among his own people. And he started back to Bethlehem. But when he came into Judah he heard that Herod's son, who was also named Herod, was now the ruler of the Jews in Judah, and he feared that this new king might be cruel like his father had been. Because of this fear Joseph journeyed on to Nazareth, in the country of Galilee, where he and Mary had lived before Jesus was born. And there he made a home for his wife and her wonderful child.

Luke 2:40–52

Nazareth, the boyhood home of Jesus, was nearly seventy miles from Jerusalem. The Jews who lived in this city could not go every week to worship God at the temple, so they built a house of worship, called a synagogue, in their home town. Here they attended religious services, and listened to the reading of the books written by Moses and by the prophets.

As a little boy Jesus lived in the humble home of Joseph, the carpenter, and played among the shavings that fell from Joseph's bench. He also liked to run about and play in the warm sunshine, as little children do today. But when he grew old enough to go to school his parents sent him to the synagogue, where other Jewish boys were taught to read and to write.

We are sure that Jesus studied hard, and that he gave careful attention to the books he read each day. These books were copies of the Psalms and of the writings of Moses, the lawgiver, and the prophets. Like other Jewish boys, he learned to repeat many of these scriptures from memory, for he never had a Bible of his own.

One spring morning after Jesus was twelve years old a company of Jews started from Nazareth to attend the Feast of the Passover, at Jerusalem. Every year since their return from Egypt, Joseph and Mary had attended this feast, and now, as usual, they were in this company. But this time they were taking with them the boy Jesus.

Other children, too, were going, and they would enjoy the long trip of nearly seventy miles much more than would their parents and grown-up friends.

As the company moved slowly along the road, other Jews from cities and villages near by joined them. And when they came to Jerusalem they met people from every part of the land. What an exciting time this must have been for the children! How wide their eyes must have opened when they saw the beautiful temple on Mount Moriah, with its wide porches and immense pillars of stone! And perhaps they stayed close by their parents during the first days of the Feast, lest they should get lost in the throng of people who daily crowded the temple courts.

Jesus enjoyed this Feast as much as did his parents and grown-up friends. Although just a child, he was beginning to realize that God was his Father, and that he must work for God. So he listened to the readings of the law, and to the words of the chief priests and scribes, who taught the Jews every day. But we are sure that he acted very much like a healthy twelve-year-old boy, for his mother did not notice how deeply interested he had been in the services at the temple.

After the Feast had ended, the company started on its homeward journey. Mary did not see her young son; but since she supposed that he was among their kinsfolk and friends, she did not feel uneasy. However, when at evening he did not come, she and Joseph began to search for him. All through the company they went, asking about Jesus; but no one had seen him that day. Then they turned with anxious faces back toward Jerusalem, and for three days they searched for their missing child.

On the third day they found him, not playing with other boys in the streets, nor learning to swim in the Pool of Siloam, but sitting in the temple among the wise teachers, and asking them questions, which they could hardly answer.

Mary was surprised when she found her boy in the temple among the wise men. She had looked every other place for him. She knew he was a boy, just a boy, and she was surprised to find him so deeply interested in the teachings of God. She came to him and said, "Son, why did you stay here when we were starting home? Your father and I have been anxiously seeking for you everywhere." Jesus answered, "Why did you seek for me? Did you not know that I must be about my Father's business?" He meant, "Why did you not know where to find me at once? For I must be about my heavenly Father's business." But Mary did not understand, though she wondered much about the meaning of his words.

The wise men in the temple had been much surprised to hear the wisdom of the boy Jesus. They had gathered around him to ask questions that only wise persons could answer. And Jesus answered them, every one.

But when Mary and Joseph came to the temple, Jesus left the teachers there and returned with his parents to Nazareth. He was an obedient child, and as the years passed by he grew into a noble young man. Not only did he learn how to explain the Scriptures, but he watched Joseph at his work until he, too, became a carpenter. And by his kind, thoughtful ways he won many friends. In this humble home in Nazareth, Jesus lived until he was about thirty years old.

THE LIFE OF JESUS

Matt. 3; Mark 1:2–11;
Luke 3:1–23; John 1:15–34

While Jesus was growing to manhood in the city of Nazareth, in Galilee, John, the son of Zacharias, was growing to manhood in the desert country of Judea. John spent much of his time alone in this desert country, listening to God's voice. And when he became a man he left his lonely home in the desert and began to tell God's words to the people.

John did not go to the cities of the land to preach God's message, but stayed in the wilderness of Judea near the River Jordan. And the people came from every part of the land to hear him speak. There had been no prophet among the Jews since the days of Malachi, more than four hundred years before, and now everybody was eager to hear this strange preacher in the wilderness tell the words that God had spoken to him. They believed he was a prophet, sent from God, and they came in great numbers to hear his words.

And John's words were indeed wonderful. He told the people that they should turn away from their sins and begin to do right, for God's kingdom was near at hand. He said that the King for whom they had been looking would soon come among them. And those who confessed their sins he baptized in the River. For this reason they called him "John the Baptist."

John taught the people who came to him that they should be unselfish, and kind to the poor. He told those who were rich to share their food and their clothing with the needy. He told those who were soldiers to harm no one, and to be contented with their wages. He tried in this way to teach them that God's kingdom would be a kingdom of love and peace, and "good will toward men," just as the angels sang to the shepherds on the night of Jesus' birth.

News of the strange preacher in the wilderness spread to even the farthest corners of the land, and everywhere the people were talking about his message. They were wondering whether John was the prophet Elijah come back to earth again, for John did not dress like other men. He wore only a rough garment woven of camel's hair, and tied about his waist with a skin girdle. And he ate the simple food that he found in the wilderness, like dried locusts and wild honey. And he was bold, like Elijah had been, and unafraid to speak the truth even to the wicked King Herod.

But when John heard about the wonderings of the people, he said, "I am the voice of one crying in the wilderness, and warning you to prepare for the coming King. After me there is coming one greater than I—so much greater that I am not worthy to unfasten his shoes. And though I baptize you with water, he shall baptize you with the Holy Spirit, sent down from heaven."

After these things happened, one day Jesus came from Nazareth to the Jordan River, where John was preaching and baptizing the people. And Jesus asked to be baptized also. John did not believe that Jesus needed to be baptized, and he said, "You are so much greater than I that I should be baptized by you. Why do you come to me?" But Jesus answered, "It is necessary that I should be baptized by you, because this is God's plan." So John took Jesus into the River and baptized him there.

When these two were coming up out of the water, suddenly the heavens opened above them and the Spirit of God, in the form of a beautiful dove, came down and sat upon Jesus' head. Then a voice from heaven said, "This is my beloved Son, in whom I am well pleased." And John knew by this sign who Jesus was; for God had told him that some day he would see the heavens open and the Spirit of God descend upon the coming King.

After this time John continued to preach, and sometimes the second King Herod heard him. Although Herod was troubled because John told him about his sins, his wife was much displeased with this fearless preacher of the wilderness. She wanted her husband, Herod, to kill him; and to please her, Herod shut John up in prison.

You remember the story about the beautiful Garden of Eden, where the first man and woman lived when the world was new. And you remember about the visit of the tempter, who came into that beautiful garden one day and persuaded Eve, the woman, to do wrong. Before that time there was no sin in the world; but after Eve listened to the tempter and obeyed his words, sin crept into her heart. And then Adam, the first man, also disobeyed God and allowed sin to creep into his heart.

Because sin found a place in the hearts of the first man and woman, sin was born in the hearts of all their children. And for this reason God sent Jesus, his dear Son, into the world, to save the people from their sins and to wash away the stains sin had made.

Satan, the tempter, knew about God's plan to save people from their sins through Jesus. And he tried to spoil God's plan just as he had done before. He tried to crowd sin into the loving heart of Jesus.

After the baptism at the Jordan River, when God's voice spoke from heaven and said, "This is my beloved Son," Jesus was led by the Spirit of God into the lonely wilderness. There he lived by himself for forty days, among the wild beasts. But God did not allow any harm to come to him.

And Satan, the tempter, found Jesus all alone in the wilderness. So he tempted him there. First in one way and then in another he tried to get Jesus to listen to his cunning plans and open his heart to let sin enter, just as Adam and

Eve had done. But Jesus would not listen.

When the forty days were ended, Jesus grew very faint and hungry, for he had eaten nothing since he came into this lonely place. And Satan remembered how he had tempted Eve to eat pleasant food, and how this temptation had caused her to listen to his words. He thought he would try the same temptation on Jesus. He said, "If you really are the Son of God, command that these stones become loaves of bread." He thought Jesus would surely yield to this temptation and try to prove that he was God's Son. But Jesus answered, "Man shall not live by bread only, but by every word of God."

Although he was hungry and faint, Jesus would not use his great power to please himself. He was willing to trust his heavenly Father to care for him in that desert place, and supply his needs as he had supplied food for Elijah. Satan soon saw that he could not cause Jesus to yield to such a temptation, so he tried another way.

Taking Jesus to the topmost part of the temple in Jerusalem, he said, "If you expect people to believe that you are really God's Son you must show some great sign. Now cast yourself down to the ground, and trust God to protect you and keep your bones from being broken; for in the Scripture he has promised that angels will bear you up and not allow any harm to befall you."

Even though Satan used Scripture words to urge Jesus to do this foolish deed, Jesus would not obey him. For Jesus knew that the Scriptures had forbidden anyone to tempt God in such a foolish manner and expect God's angels to help him. And again Satan saw that his plan had failed.

The third time Satan brought his greatest temptation. He took Jesus to the top of a high mountain and caused him to see all the kingdoms of the world. "These great kingdoms are mine," said the tempter, "and I can give them to anyone I choose. Now I will give them to you if only you will fall down and worship me."

But Jesus knew that Satan's words were not true. He knew that Satan had told falsehoods to Eve in the beautiful Garden of Eden. Now he said, "Get away from me, you evil one! For it is written in the Scriptures that the Lord God is the only Being who should be worshiped."

Then Satan left Jesus alone; for he could find no way to crowd sin into the pure heart of the Son of God. And when he went away the angels came from heaven and supplied Jesus' needs. How they must have rejoiced because the Savior had gained such a victory over the evil one!

And Jesus was tempted in every way that people on the earth are tempted; still he did no wrong. By his temptations he was made to understand how people feel when Satan whispers to their hearts and urges them to sin, and he understood how to help those people when they call upon him in prayer.

John 1:35–51

Many people who heard John preach by the riverside believed his words, and they began to look for the coming of the King from heaven. From day to day they waited, eager to hear the glad news that the King had arrived. They believed that he would set up a kingdom in Judea, like the kingdom of David had been. And they believed that the Jews would be the favored people in this great kingdom.

One day after Jesus had returned from the lonely wilderness, John the Baptist saw him walking along the road near the river. And John cried out, "Behold the Lamb of God, who bears the sin of the world!"

Two young men from Galilee were with John that day and heard him speak. These young men had been disciples, or learners, of John, for they were interested in the teachings of God. When they heard John's words concerning Jesus, the Lamb of God, they turned at once to follow this wonderful person. Perhaps they wondered why John had called him the "Lamb of God." And perhaps they wondered how he could bear the sin of the world.

Jesus knew these young men were following him, so he stopped and called to them. He asked what they wanted of him, and they answered, "Master, where do you dwell?" Then Jesus took them with him and talked with them all that day.

We do not know what Jesus told those men, but we do know that his words proved to their minds that he was the King, or Messiah, for whom the Jews were looking. How glad they were because they had found him!

One of those young men was Andrew, who afterward became a disciple of Jesus. Just as soon as he believed that Jesus was the promised King he remembered how eagerly his brother, Simon, was waiting to see this great person, too. So he hurried at once to find Simon and bring him to Jesus.

Both Simon and Andrew lived by the seaside in Galilee, but at this time they were numbered among the many people who daily sat listening to the words of the strange preacher in the wilderness. Never had they heard such wonderful teaching before, and they were sure that John was a prophet. But Jesus' words had convinced Andrew that he had found a new teacher who was even greater than John. So he called Simon aside from the multitude and said, "Come with me, for we have found the Messiah!"

When Jesus saw the two brothers coming to his lodging place he looked at Simon and said, "You are Simon, the son of Jona, but you shall be called Peter." Simon wondered how Jesus knew so much about him, but after he listened to Jesus' words he, too, believed that the long-looked-for King of the Jews had come. And he followed Jesus with his brother Andrew.

On the next day Jesus began his journey back to his home country in Galilee, and these men went with him. As they went they met a man named Philip, who lived in the same town as Simon and Andrew lived in. Jesus called Philip to follow him, too, and Philip obeyed. As he walked along the road with Jesus and the other followers Philip listened in wonder to the wise sayings of his newfound friend. He had longed for the coming of the Messiah, and now he, too, believed that Jesus was the promised Savior and King.

Philip had a neighbor named Nathaniel who had often talked with him about the glorious time soon coming when the King of the Jews would appear. And now he ran to tell Nathaniel about Jesus. He knew how greatly Nathaniel longed to see the coming King, and he called to him, saying, "We have found him, of whom Moses in the law, and the prophets, did write, Jesus of Nazareth."

Nathaniel knew the Scriptures, and he did not believe that the King of the Jews would come from Nazareth, for the prophets had said he would be born in Bethlehem. So he said to Philip, "Can any good thing come out of Nazareth?" But Philip answered, "Come and see."

Because Philip was so eager, Nathaniel rose and followed him. When they came near, Jesus saw Nathaniel, and he said, "Behold an Israelite indeed, in whom is no guile!"

"How do you know me?" he asked astonished, and Jesus answered, "Before Philip called you, when you were under the fig tree, I saw you."

What Nathaniel had been doing under the fig tree we can only guess, but he may have been kneeling there and praying that God would hasten the coming of the promised King. When he heard Jesus' answer, he was filled with wonder and surprise that Jesus could know what he had been doing and where he had been staying before Philip called him. At once he believed that only God can see all things, and can reveal them to men, so he exclaimed joyfully, "Master, you are the Son of God! You are the King of Israel!"

Jesus replied, "Do you believe just because I said I saw you under the fig tree? You shall see greater things than these. Some day you shall see the heavens open, and the angels of God all about the Son of man."

John 2:1–11

n Cana, a little town of Galilee, lived some friends of Jesus and his mother. One day these friends invited Jesus, his mother, and his followers to attend a wedding in their home. They invited many other people also, and prepared a feast for them.

Perhaps these people were poor; for they had not prepared enough wine for all the people who came to the wedding. And before the close of the feast the wine was all gone.

Mary, the mother of Jesus, saw that the wine had all been used, and she called Jesus aside to tell him about it. She knew of his wonderful power, and she believed he could surely help in a time like this. Then she told the servants who waited at the tables to do whatever Jesus might command them, for she expected him to supply the need in some wonderful manner.

In every Jewish home there were large vessels, called water-pots, which the people kept filled with water to use in washing their hands and their feet. The Jews were very careful to keep themselves clean from dust and dirt, and because they walked about everywhere with only sandals on their feet they needed often to wash. In this home where the wedding feast was being held, six large water-pots of stone were kept for this purpose.

Jesus called the servants and told them to fill the water-pots with water. And remembering his mother's instructions to them, the servants drew water and filled the vessels to the brim. Then Jesus told them to draw out from the vessels and fill their wine pitchers again. When they obeyed they saw that wine flowed from the vessels they had just filled with water.

At these Jewish feasts one man was chosen to be the governor, or ruler of the feast. He tasted the food and the wine before it was placed on the tables to serve the people. Jesus told the servants to take this wine to the governor and have him taste it, just as he had tasted the first wine that had been served to the guests.

Now the governor did not know what Jesus had done. He did not know that the other wine had all been used and there was no more to be had. When he tasted the wine which Jesus had made from water he was surprised because it was so much better than the first wine that had been served. Calling the young man who had just been married, the governor said, "At other wedding feasts the best wine is served first, but you have kept the best until the last of the feast."

This was the first miracle Jesus performed, and it showed his willingness to help people who are in need. When the men who followed him saw what he had done they believed in him, for they knew that no man could change water into wine as he did.

John 2: 13–3:21

The time had come again for the yearly Passover Feast in Jerusalem, and from every part of the land groups of people came flocking to attend this great religious meeting.

In one of these groups were Jesus and his friends, Andrew, Simon, Philip, and Nathaniel. These men were also called his disciples, or learners; for they often went with him from one place to another to learn more about his wonderful teachings.

You remember that only the priests were allowed to enter the rooms of the temple, and that the people who went there to worship stood in the courts outside the rooms and prayed while the priests offered sacrifices upon the altars.

When Jesus came with his disciples and friends to attend the Feast of the Passover, he found much disorder in the court where the people were supposed to worship God. This beautiful court looked more like a marketplace than like a house of prayer, for men had brought oxen and sheep and doves in there to sell as sacrifices to those who came from distant country places to worship God.

And other men, who were called money-changers, were sitting by small tables exchanging pieces of silver money, called half-shekels, for the coins people brought from distant lands. Every Jew, we are told, who was twenty years old or older, gave one of these half-shekels to the priests each year to buy sacrifices and to supply other needs in the temple worship. No other coins except half-shekels could be received by the priests, so the Jews who came from other lands had to exchange their coins for half-shekels before they could pay their dues to the priests.

Jesus was grieved to see the disorder in the temple court. He knew that worshipers could not enjoy praying in such a noisy place, where buying and selling and money-exchanging were going on around them. So he made a whip by tying small cords together, and then he drove out the oxen and sheep and the men who kept them. He even upset the tables of the money-changers, and he told them that his Father's house was a place of prayer and should not be used for a marketplace.

No doubt other people had been grieved to see the disorder in the temple court at the time of the Passover feast. But none of them had ever dared to do as Jesus did at this time. None of them had courage enough to try to correct this great evil.

But not all of the Jews were pleased to see Jesus drive the money-changers and the owners of the oxen and sheep and doves into the streets outside the temple. Some of them came to Jesus and asked him for a sign to prove that he was some great man, with authority to do such things. But Jesus knew they would not accept him even when they should see a sign, so he answered, "Destroy this temple, and in three days I will raise it." By this, Jesus meant that should they destroy his body, he would raise up from the dead after three days. But the Jews did not understand, and they thought he meant the temple on Mount Moriah, which Herod, the king, had rebuilt for them. They said, "Many years were spent in building this temple, and you say you could rebuild it in three days!" Then they shook their heads doubtfully and walked away, for they did not believe his words.

At this Feast, Jesus began to teach the people and to do miracles among them. And many believed in him when they heard his words and saw the great works which no other man could do.

One of those who believed in Jesus was a ruler among the Jews, a Pharisee. His name was Nicodemus, and he was a very rich man. There were many Pharisees among the Jewish rulers, and these men were proud and unwilling to accept either John the Baptist or Jesus as being teachers sent from God. They themselves wished to be the religious leaders of the Jews and they despised humble men like John and Jesus. But Nicodemus was not like his proud friends. He heard Jesus teach the people who had come to worship at the Feast, and he believed that surely Jesus was some great man.

While the other Pharisees were finding fault with Jesus, Nicodemus longed to hear more of his teachings. So one night he came to the place where Jesus stayed while he was in Jerusalem, and asked to have a talk with this man from Galilee.

Jesus received Nicodemus gladly, and talked to him about the kingdom of God. He told this ruler that no man could enter God's kingdom unless he should be born again. Nicodemus wondered how this could be possible, so Jesus explained to him the secret of the new birth, which we call a change of heart. Never before had this wise ruler of the Jews heard such strange words, and he listened wonderingly while Jesus told about the great love of God. "This love," said Jesus, "caused God to give his only Son that whoever believes in him may not die because of sin, but have life forevermore."

Then Jesus reminded Nicodemus of the story of Moses in the wilderness when the people had sinned and God had sent fiery snakes into their camp. Nicodemus remembered the story, and Jesus said, "Just as those people who were about to die from the snake bites found relief from their pain by looking at the brass snake that Moses put up on a pole in their camp, so the people who have sin in their hearts may find relief from sin by looking at the Son of man, who shall be raised up among them." Nicodemus did not understand that Jesus was speaking about the cruel way in which he should some time be put to death to save the people from their sins. But Nicodemus did believe more strongly than ever that Jesus was a great teacher who had come down from heaven to dwell among men.

John 4:1–43

Between Judea and Galilee was a little country called Samaria. This country used to belong to the kingdom of Israel; but when the Israelites were carried away as captives by the king of Assyria, strangers from other lands came into that country and made their homes.

These strangers learned about the God of the Israelites, but they never worshiped God at the temple in Jerusalem. Instead, they built a temple in their country and worshiped there. They became bitter enemies of the Jews, and at the time of Jesus they were still despised by the Jews. In going to or returning from Jerusalem, the Jews of Galilee usually would not take the shorter road, through Samaria, but would travel the long road, which led first to and across the Jordan River, then along the border of the land where the people lived whom they despised.

Although Jesus was a Jew he did not share the bitter feeling of the Jews toward the people of Samaria, who were called Samaritans. He knew they were just as precious in the eyes of God as were any other people, and he longed to teach them about the kingdom of heaven. He did not mind walking through their country on his journey back to his home in Nazareth.

Because Jesus wished to take the shorter road, through Samaria, his disciples were willing to go that way, too, in order to be with him. So they journeyed together as far as a little city called Sychar.

Near the city was a wayside well, which had been dug hundreds of years before probably by Jacob, the grandson of Abraham. And in honor of him it was still called Jacob's well. When they reached this well, Jesus was tired, and sat down by it to rest from his long walk. His disciples went on to the city to buy food, leaving him there alone.

Presently a woman from Sychar came down to the well to draw some water. She glanced at the stranger sitting there and saw that he was a Jew. Knowing that Jews paid no attention to Samaritans, she passed by and hurried to lower her water jug with the long rope that she had brought. When the jug was filled she drew it up and was ready to start back to the city, when Jesus asked for a drink.

Surprised at his request, the woman answered, "How is it that you, being a Jew, will ask a drink of me, a woman of

Samaria, for the Jews have no dealings with the Samaritans?"

Jesus replied, "If you knew who it is who asks a drink from your jug of sparkling water, you would ask of him and he would give you living water to drink."

These words aroused the interest of the woman at once. Who could this stranger be? she wondered. She knew he was not like other Jews, for they would rather suffer from thirst than ask a favor of a Samaritan. So she said, "Sir, this well is deep and you have no rope to draw out the water, how then could you give me living water to drink? Are you greater than Jacob, who gave us this well, and drank of it himself, and his cattle?"

"Whoever drinks of this water in Jacob's well becomes thirsty and returns again and again for more," answered Jesus, "but the living water that I give does not come from such a well. It bubbles up like a continual spring within one, so that one never grows thirsty again."

Now the woman was an eager listener. She did not know that the living water of which Jesus spoke was his free gift of salvation to all people, and she said, "Sir, I want that kind of water so that I shall not need to return and refill my water jug in this tiresome way."

Jesus saw that she was interested, so he began to talk to her about her sins. He knew she was a very sinful woman, and he told her about some wrong things that she had done. She wondered how he, a stranger, could know these things. He seemed to see her thoughts and to read them all. "You are a prophet," she exclaimed.

Although this woman was a sinner, she wondered often whether God was more pleased with the religion of the Jews than with the religion of her own people, the Samaritans. Now she asked Jesus whether people should worship God in Jerusalem or in the temple of the Samaritans.

Jesus answered that God had planned to bring salvation through the Jews, but he said the time had come when true worshipers need no longer go up to Jerusalem, for they might pray to God everywhere and worship him. "God is not found in only one place," he said, "for God is a Spirit. And those who worship him in the right way must believe that he is a Spirit."

Then the woman said, "I know the Messiah is coming from God, and when he comes he will tell us everything."

"I am that Messiah," answered Jesus, and the woman looked in joy and wonder upon him. But at that moment the disciples returned from the city bringing food to eat, so she turned away and, leaving her water jug, ran back to tell her friends about the wonderful stranger whom she had met at the well.

The disciples wondered why Jesus would talk with a despised woman of the Samaritans; but they did not ask him any questions. They brought food to him, and when he refused to eat they urged him. Then he said to them, "I have food to eat that you know nothing about." They asked each other, "Has some one brought food to him while we were away?" But Jesus knew their questionings, so he said, "My sustenance is to do the will of my Father, who has sent me into the world."

When the woman reached the city she went into the streets and told the people about Jesus, the stranger who had understood all about her life. "He told me all the things that

I ever did. Is not he the Messiah?" she asked. And the people decided to see this man for themselves, so they went with her to Jacob's well.

Jesus talked with the Samaritans about the things of God, and they invited him to stay in their city and teach them more of these wonderful truths. He spent two days in Sychar, teaching the people. Then he went on his way to Nazareth, leaving behind him some believers among the Samaritans.

John 4:45–54

Many people who lived in the country of Galilee were eager to see Jesus. They had heard about his first miracle at Cana, where he turned water into wine, and they had also heard about his teachings and his miracles performed in Jerusalem during the Feast of the Passover. Now when he left Sychar and returned with his disciples to their country, the news of his coming spread rapidly from one city to another, and the Galilean people hoped he would come to their cities and perform miracles among them, too.

But one man did not wait until Jesus should come to his home city before going out to see him. This man lived in Capernaum, a city that had been built on the shore of the Sea of Galilee. He was one of the rulers in that city, and he was also called a nobleman. In the eyes of the poor who lived near his home he was a great man indeed, for he did not despise them, as did many of the rulers of the Jews.

Sorrow had come into the home of this nobleman, his

little son lay sick with a burning fever, and the doctors could not make him well. Hearing of Jesus, the nobleman decided to seek this wonderful prophet and beg him to come to Capernaum to heal his child. So he left his home one night and hurried to Cana, where Jesus was.

When the nobleman found the place where Jesus was stopping, he called to see the wonderful prophet of Galilee. He told Jesus about his sick child lying at home at the point of death, and he asked Jesus to go with him to Capernaum to heal the child. But Jesus answered, "Unless you see signs and wonders you will not believe that I am sent of God."

The nobleman was very much in earnest. He cried out, "Sir, if you do not come down at once, my little son will be dead when we reach home." Then Jesus spoke kindly to this distressed father. He said, "Return to your home without me, for your son will not die."

The nobleman believed Jesus' words and turned back to Capernaum. He did not fear any longer that death would snatch his dear child away from his loving care, for Jesus had said that the child should be well again. When he came near to Capernaum, his servants came to meet him with glad tidings. They said, "Your son is no longer sick."

"At what time," asked the nobleman, "did he begin to get well?" And the servants replied, "His fever left him yesterday at the seventh hour of the day." The ruler knew that Jesus had spoken to him at that very hour, and he believed surely that it was the power of this prophet that had saved the life of his child. Not only this nobleman, but all his household, too, believed in Jesus when they heard about the healing of the sick boy.

A sad day had come for Nazareth, the city where Jesus had lived since his babyhood years. And this sad day had come on the Sabbath. The Jews from different parts of the city were gathering in their house of worship, the synagogue. Among their number was Jesus, for he had returned from his visit in Cana. Always while he lived in Nazareth he went every Sabbath day to the services at the synagogue, where he heard God's words read from the books of the law and of the prophets.

Now, Jesus was no longer just an ordinary person among the other Jews of Nazareth, for they had heard about his teachings in other cities and they wished to hear for themselves what this son of the carpenter Joseph would say. So when the time came for the services to begin, Jesus stood up to read to the people, and the minister of the synagogue brought to him the book that the prophet Isaiah had written long years before. Jesus found where Isaiah wrote the prophecy concerning the Messiah, and he read Isaiah's prophecy to the people. These are some of the words he read:

> "The Spirit of the Lord is upon me,
> Because he hath anointed me to preach the
> gospel to the poor;
> He has sent me to heal the broken-hearted,
> To preach deliverance to the captives,
> And recovering of sight to the blind,
> To set at liberty them that are bruised,
> To preach the acceptable year of the Lord."

After reading these words, Jesus closed the book, gave it back to the minister, and sat down. Then everyone in the synagogue looked at him, expecting to hear him speak; for the speaker in the synagogue always stood up to read God's words and sat down to explain the meaning of what he had read.

Among those who listened to Jesus that day were his neighbors who had known him nearly all his lifetime. Proud men they were, unwilling that the carpenter's son should teach them new truths. They had heard of the miracles that Jesus performed in Cana and in Capernaum, the city by the seashore. But they did not believe that Jesus was the promised King of the Jews. They knew he was only a poor man, and they did not respect him for being great and good.

But those proud men were surprised when they heard Jesus' words. They did not know he could speak so well; they did not know that he was the greatest teacher who had ever spoken to men. For a while they listened very carefully; then Jesus told them that Isaiah's words were fulfilled by his coming to preach the gospel to the poor and to do other wonderful things that Isaiah had promised. "How can this be true?" they asked of each other, "for is not this Joseph's son?"

Jesus knew they would not receive his words and believe them. He told them that no prophet was honored by his own people. And he reminded them of the time when Elijah, the prophet, ran away from Israel to hide in the home of a poor widow who lived in a heathen land. Because this poor widow cared for God's prophet, God took care of her. He also told them about the heathen leper, Naaman, who was healed by God's power when he obeyed Elisha's words, although many Israelites had leprosy and were never healed.

The proud men of Nazareth quickly objected to these words of Jesus, although they were true happenings among the Jews long before. They believed that Jesus was trying to show them how God cared for other people besides the Jews, and they did not like to hear such words. So they refused to listen longer to his teachings, and the service at the synagogue broke up in great disorder. The leading men ran to Jesus and took hold of him roughly and drew him outside their synagogue. Then a mob of angry people followed, wishing to see Jesus punished because he had spoken these words to them.

This mob led Jesus to the top of the high hill upon which Nazareth was built, intending to throw him down upon the sharp rocks in the canon below But the time had not yet come when Jesus should die for the sins of the people, and therefore they could not carry out their wicked intention. He simply walked quietly through the midst of the excited throng. No one seized hold of him again, and he left them and went away to live in Capernaum, the city by the Sea of Galilee.

The men of Nazareth did not know what a terrible deed they had tried to do that day; they did not know that their foolish pride had caused them to drive right out of their midst the gift which God had sent from heaven to earth. And because they refused to believe in Jesus as the one of whom Isaiah had written, they never received the gift of salvation, which Jesus brought to the people.

A fter a time, Jesus went to live in Capernaum near his disciples. Here he taught in the synagogue on the Sabbath days, and the people of Capernaum were glad to listen to his words. He did not teach them as did their usual Jewish teachers, repeating the same words again and again each time he spoke, but always his words sounded new, and just as if God were speaking to the people.

One morning, two of the disciples, Andrew and Simon, were busy at work in their fishing boats on the Sea of Galilee when they saw Jesus walking along the shore. He called to them, and they left their boats and followed him. Farther along they saw two other fishermen in a ship mending their torn nets. These men were brothers, and their names were James and John. They were partners in the fishing business with Simon and Andrew, and when they saw their partners following Jesus they ceased their work, wondering where Simon and Andrew were going. Jesus called them also, and they left their ship at once in the care of their father and the servants who were helping mend the nets.

Taking these four fishermen with him, Jesus returned to the city. And on the next Sabbath day they went with him into the synagogue, where many people had come to hear his words.

Among the crowd who had gathered that day in the synagogue was one man in whom Satan had put a very bad spirit. This bad spirit caused the man to cry aloud when he saw

Jesus, and say, "Let us alone! What do we have to do with you, Jesus of Nazareth? I know you are the Holy One from God."

Jesus was not pleased to have a spirit of Satan speak to him like this. So he commanded the bad spirit to come out of the man. And the spirit threw the poor man on the floor before all the people, tearing him and crying with a wicked cry. But at Jesus' command the bad spirit had to leave the man; for Jesus has power over all the power of Satan, to cast out the evil spirits that come to dwell in people.

When those standing by saw what Jesus had done, they were greatly astonished. Never before had they seen anyone with power to rebuke the evil spirits. They said to each other, "What thing is this? What new doctrine is this? For Jesus even dares to command evil spirits and they must obey him!"

Quickly the news of this wonderful happening in the synagogue spread to every part of the city, and everybody became interested in the great teacher who had lately come to live among them. They were so glad he had come, and they wished to carry their suffering friends and loved ones to him that he might cure them of their sicknesses and diseases. So they began to plan how they might do this.

Jesus had gone with his disciples from the synagogue to the home of Simon and Andrew. When they arrived they heard that Simon's mother-in-law was lying sick with fever. So they told Jesus about her, and brought him into the room where she lay suffering. Jesus came to her bedside, and taking hold of her hand he lifted her up. At that very moment the fever departed and strength came into her body again.

She rose from her bed and helped to prepare food for the disciples and their wonderful teacher.

At sunset the Sabbath day closed for the Jews and then they were free to begin their work again, for they never did any work on the Sabbath. When sunset came on this day of rest Simon and Andrew were surprised to see throngs of people coming toward their home. From every direction the people were coming, some with crippled friends leaning on their arms, and others with blind friends walking by their side. Still others were carrying cots on which lay their sick children or other relatives, and all of them were coming to ask Jesus to drive away the sicknesses and diseases and to make their friends and loved ones well again.

What a busy time followed! Jesus was glad to help these poor sufferers and to make them well. He touched them, one by one, and they were healed. He even cast out many evil spirits from the people who had come.

Finally the last group of happy friends departed from the doorstep, and Jesus lay down to sleep in Simon's house. How very tired he must have been! But after sleeping only a few hours he rose up quietly and left the city. He sought for a place where he might be all alone to talk with his heavenly Father, for often he prayed earnestly to God for strength and help to do the great work that he had to do.

When daylight broke, people began coming again to Simon's home, asking for Jesus. But Jesus was not there. Simon and his friends began to search for Jesus, and they found him at his place of prayer. They told him about the anxious seekers who had come early to find him again, and Jesus said, "I must preach the kingdom of God in other cities also, for I am sent to do this great work." So the disciples went with him to visit other cities in Galilee, and Jesus taught in the synagogues of those cities and cast out evil spirits, as he had done in Capernaum. And many people believed in him.

After some time he returned again to Capernaum, and his disciples went back to their work as fishermen. But Jesus continued to teach the people who came to hear his words. One day he went out to the seaside where his disciples were at work, washing their nets. Many people saw him leave the city, and they followed. Soon a great crowd gathered on the shore, eager to hear him preach. So Jesus asked permission to sit in Simon's ship and speak to the people who stood on the shore.

When Jesus finished speaking he told Simon to row out into the deep water and lower his net to catch some fish. Simon replied, "Master, we have fished all night and have caught nothing; however, if you wish we will try again." So they rowed away from the land and let down their nets once more. This time a great many fishes quickly swam into the net and were caught. Simon and Andrew could not draw them out of the water alone, for their net began to break with the weight of the many fishes. They signaled for their partners, James and John, and the four men worked together. They had never seen so many fishes in one net before. Soon the ship was filled, and they began to put more fish in the second ship. Finally both ships began to sink with the weight of the fishes and the men.

Now, the fishermen knew that Jesus had performed a miracle by causing so many fish to be in the net. Simon fell down at Jesus' knees and cried, "Leave me, O Lord, for I am a sinful man and am not worthy of all you have given to us here." But Jesus was not ready to leave Simon. He answered, "Do not be afraid, for hereafter you shall catch men." And Simon understood from Jesus' words that he must leave his fishing business and follow the Master everywhere he went. So when the fishers made their way to the shore they forsook their ships and walked with Jesus from one city to another, helping him and learning daily more and more about the kingdom of God.

Matt. 9:9–13; Mark 2:14–17;
Luke 5:27–32

I n the land where Jesus lived there was among the Jews one class of people whom all other Jews despised. This class was the publicans, or tax-gatherers, who worked for the Roman government.

The Jews hated the Roman government because they wished to be an independent nation, having a Jewish ruler over them. For this reason they were eagerly awaiting the time when the kingdom of God should come. They believed the kingdom of God would be set up in the same country as that in which David used to live and rule. And they expected to become the greatest people in all the world when that kingdom should be set up. Any Jew who was friendly with the Roman government they hated, because they thought he was not being true to his own nation.

The Jews who were more friendly toward the Romans, and who worked for the Roman government, were called publicans. They took the tax money from the Jews, which the ruler at Rome demanded of them. And often they took more money than the Roman ruler called for. In this manner they stole from the people, and became very rich themselves. And the people hated them, and called them sinners.

Not all the publicans robbed the people by asking too much tax money from them. But because many of them did this, the people believed that all of them were guilty of such wrong-doing. And they called every publican a sinner.

One day while Jesus was passing along a street in the city

of Capernaum he saw a man named Matthew sitting at a publican's table, taking the tax money from the people. Although Matthew was a publican, whom other Jews despised, Jesus saw the heart of this man and he knew Matthew would make a good disciple. So he called this publican to follow him, and Matthew gladly left his money table and obeyed the call.

Matthew was also called Levi, for the Jews sometimes had two names. And after he began to follow Jesus he remembered his friends of other days. He believed they, too, would be glad to see Jesus and to hear his words. So Matthew prepared a great feast or banquet and called many of his publican friends to the feast. He invited other people too, who were despised and called sinners, and then he brought Jesus and the other disciples to the feast.

The scribes and Pharisees also came to Matthew's house that day, though they had not been invited to the feast. They stood about in the courtyard or even in the large dining hall, looking on and talking to each other about what they saw. This was not so rude as it seems, for this was a custom among those people and Matthew was not at all surprised when they came.

These onlookers began to find fault when they saw Jesus sitting among the publicans and sinners. They felt themselves too good to keep company with despised folk, and they were surprised that Jesus should eat with Matthew and his friends. So they called Jesus' disciples aside and asked, "How is it that your Master eats and drinks with publicans and sinners?"

Jesus heard the questioning of these fault-finders, and he

said to them, "It is not healthy people who need to call for the services of a doctor, but people who are sick. And so I have not come to call righteous people, but I have come to call sinners to repent." He knew the scribes and Pharisees believed themselves to be too righteous to need repentance, but he knew the publicans and sinners realized that they were not pleasing God. And they would listen to Jesus' words, and humble their hearts. Many of them would gladly forsake their sins and follow Jesus to learn of him.

Matthew, the publican, became a very useful man for God. It was he who wrote the book called the "Gospel According to Matthew," in the New Testament. And in this writing he gives us more of the words that Jesus spoke than do any other of the gospel writers.

Matt. 10:2–4; Mark 3:13–19;
Luke 6:12–16

Many people besides Matthew, the publican, followed Jesus. His teachings were so wonderful that others wished to be learners, or disciples, of him, and so they followed in his company from one place to another.

But the time came when Jesus wished to choose from among their number twelve men whom he could prepare to help in his great work. These men he wished to send out to places where he had never yet been, and have them preach to the people in those places about the kingdom of God.

Although Jesus could see the hearts of all men, yet he felt that he needed help from God to know which of his followers he should choose to be among his twelve helpers. So one night he went away quietly and climbed up the slope of a mountain, where no one would be near to disturb him. There he knelt down to pray, and all night he prayed to God for help and wisdom, and for strength to do his work.

When morning light returned Jesus was ready to choose his helpers, so he left his place of prayer and joined the company of disciples who were waiting in the valley for his coming. From them he chose Simon whom he called Peter, and Andrew, the brother who first brought Simon to Jesus. Then he chose James and John, the fishermen who had been partners with Simon and Andrew at the seaside. Afterward he chose Matthew, the publican, and Philip and Nathaniel, of Capernaum, and Thomas, and another James, who was the son of Alphæus, and another Simon, also called Zelotes, then Judas the brother of James, and last of all Judas Iscariot.

To these twelve men Jesus gave power to cure diseases and to cast out evil. He also appointed them to preach the kingdom of God. And he called them his apostles, which means those who are sent out. Because he sent them out to preach to other men.

Of these twelve apostles we read the most about Simon Peter, James, John, Andrew, Matthew, Philip, and Thomas. Little mention is made of the others, except of Judas Iscariot, who near the end of Jesus' ministry became untrue and betrayed Jesus by selling him for money.

Matt. 5–7; Luke 6:17–49

After Jesus had chosen his twelve apostles, who were still called disciples, he took them apart from the multitude to teach them how to do his great work. Up the side of the mountain they went together, and there Jesus sat down. His disciples stood near and he spoke to them. Other people also climbed the mountain to listen to the great sermon Jesus preached that day.

In the beginning of his sermon Jesus said:"Blessed are the poor in spirit, for theirs is the kingdom of heaven." Perhaps he had been thinking about the proud spirits of the scribes and Pharisees. He knew that proud spirits will never receive his words and learn how to enter the kingdom of God. But people who are humble and who do not believe themselves to be righteous without God's help he called poor in spirit, and he said they are blessed because to them shall be given the kingdom of God, for which all Jews were seeking.

He also said: "Blessed are they that mourn, for they shall be comforted." These words sounded strange to the listeners, for they had never thought that blessings belonged to those who are grieving because of troubles and sorrows. They did not realize how God loves to comfort the weary and sad.

"Blessed are the meek," said Jesus next, "for they shall inherit the earth." By these words he meant that gentle people who do not lose their temper and allow thoughts of discontent to fill their minds will be happy and will enjoy the blessings God gives to all men.

Then Jesus said, "Blessed are they who hunger and thirst after righteousness, for they shall be filled." Perhaps he was thinking again of the proud Pharisees, who believed they were righteous in themselves and therefore did not need to repent of their sins and seek the righteousness of God. Only those are blessed with God's righteousness who long for it as earnestly as they wish for food and drink to satisfy their appetites.

"Blessed are they who show mercy to others," said Jesus, "for mercy shall be shown to them. And blessed are they who have pure hearts, for they shall see God. And blessed are they who make peace among men, for they shall be called the children of God." These words the disciples understood, for they knew God will surely bless people who show mercy, and people who will not allow sin to enter their hearts, and people who bring peace where trouble is.

Then Jesus said: "Blessed are they who are persecuted for the sake of righteousness; for theirs is the kingdom of heaven." These words sounded strange, for people who are persecuted are greatly troubled, and the disciples may have wondered how the kingdom of God could belong to them when trouble was filling their lives. But afterward they learned how people who are being persecuted for the sake of righteousness can be blessed as citizens of the kingdom of heaven. And after Jesus had been crucified and had risen from the dead, they themselves learned what it means to be persecuted for the sake of righteousness.

Jesus said that those who are so persecuted should rejoice and be very glad, because there is a great reward awaiting them in heaven.

In this wonderful sermon Jesus told the people how Christians should live. He taught them how Christians should pray, and how they should treat their enemies and their friends. He told them, too, about God's love and care for those who trust him.

At the close of his long sermon Jesus said: "Those who hear my words and do them are like the man who builds his house on a foundation of rock. When the winds blow and the rain falls fast, that foundation of rock will stand firm, and the house will not fall. But those who hear my words and do not obey them are like the man who builds his house on a foundation of sand. When the winds blow and the rain falls fast, that sandy foundation will be washed out from beneath the building, and the house will fall."

Jesus meant by these words that people who hear and obey his teachings will be saved. And when the storm of the judgment day comes they will be safe from harm. But people who hear his teachings and refuse to obey them will not be safe when the storm of the judgment day comes upon them.

When Jesus ended his sermon, the people looked at each other in surprise. They knew his teachings were more wonderful than the teachings of Moses and of the scribes and Pharisees. They wondered who could obey such commands as these: "Love your enemies." "Pray for them who treat you wrongly." "Do good to them who hate you." But they knew that Jesus' words sounded as though they were the words of God, and by and by many of them learned that even the hardest commands could be obeyed by those who truly love the Lord.

Matt. 8:1–4; Mark 1:40–45;
Luke 5:12–16

When Jesus and his twelve disciples came down from the mountain, a great multitude of people followed them. These people had come from cities and villages in every part of Galilee, and some had come even from Jerusalem and from country places in Judea.

Near this great multitude stood one poor man who had heard of Jesus' power to work miracles. And he needed, oh, so much, to have a miracle performed in his body, for the terrible disease of leprosy had fastened on him and was eating his flesh. He was not allowed to live among his friends and relatives, for fear they might become lepers also. He was not allowed to come very close to any one who was not a leper. And what an unhappy life he lived!

When the poor leper saw Jesus and his disciples coming down the mountainside, he thought, "I wonder if this Jesus will heal me." He decided to try him, so he ran to Jesus and knelt down on the ground at Jesus' feet, worshiping him. Then he said, "If you are willing, I know you can make me well from this terrible leprosy."

Jesus looked on the poor man kneeling before him, and great pity filled his heart. He knew how this man was dying, by inches, of the dreaded leprosy, which no doctors could cure. He knew about the unhappy days this poor man spent away from his own home and loved ones. He knew, too, how careful every one was to keep away from a leprous person for fear he might become a leper also.

Jesus was not afraid to touch the poor leper. He reached out his hand kindly and said, "I am willing; you may be healed now." And at that moment the leprosy left the poor man's body and new skin came upon his flesh.

The man sprang quickly to his feet, and the weary look had vanished from his eyes. Now he was well! How thankful he felt. No doubt the great change seemed too good to believe. But he saw how the leprosy was gone, and he knew Jesus had touched him and had sent healing power through his body.

In the law of God that Moses gave to the people, he commanded that lepers should offer sacrifices of thanksgiving to God when their leprosy was healed. So Jesus reminded the man of this command, and told him to go to the priests in Jerusalem and make an offering to God. And he asked the man to tell no one about the healing.

But soon the news of this great miracle spread over the countryside, and everyone was talking about it. The poor man had been so glad that he had told his friends what Jesus had done for him. And his friends told their friends, and so the news spread far and wide. And many people left their homes and rushed into the country to see the wonderful person who by his word and by the touch of his hand could drive away the leprosy from a man whose body was full of the dreadful disease.

Matt. 21:1–11; Mark 11:1–11;
Luke 19:29–40; John 12:12–19

A time of great excitement was on. People were flocking out of the city gate and hurrying along the road that led down the valley and up the slope of Mount Olivet, just outside of Jerusalem. They were rushing out to meet Jesus, of whom they had heard such great things.

Many of these people were strangers in Jerusalem. They had just come to attend the Feast of the Passover, and they had heard about the wonderful miracles Jesus performed. Others lived in Jerusalem and they had heard how Jesus raised a man from the dead, so they, too, were eager to see him again. As they went they took branches of palm trees with which to wave him a welcome when they should meet him.

On the morning of that same day Jesus had sent two of his disciples to a village near Bethany to loose a colt that they should find tied. He had told them to bring this colt to him, and if the owners should question why they untied the colt they should answer, "The Lord has need of this colt today." And the disciples had gone and found the colt tied by the roadside, and they had told the owners the message which Jesus sent. And the owners had let them take the colt and bring it to Jesus.

Then the disciples had spread their garments on the colt's back and had set Jesus on it, while others threw their clothes along the road for Jesus to ride over. And as the crowd from Jerusalem came near to the Mount of Olives, the company that followed from Bethany began to shout, "Blessed is the King who is coming in the name of the Lord! Peace in heaven, and glory in the highest!"

The people who came out of Jerusalem met Jesus and his disciples on the slope of the Mount of Olives. They heard those who followed Jesus shout praises to him, and they too waved their palms and rejoiced, saying, "Hosanna! Blessed is the King of Israel who comes in the name of the Lord!" Some threw their palms in the road for him to ride over, and all along the highway they stood, rejoicing greatly and praising God.

In the crowd were some Pharisees who had not come to rejoice but to find fault. When they heard the people shouting they came to Jesus and said, "Master, cause these people to cease shouting." But Jesus answered, "If they should be still the stones by the roadside would immediately cry out." Jesus knew the time had come when the prophecy of Zechariah should be fulfilled, for Zechariah had said concerning this very time:

> "Rejoice greatly, O daughter of Zion;
> Shout, O daughter of Jerusalem:
> Behold, your King comes unto you:

He is just, and having salvation;
Lowly, and riding upon a colt."

So the crowd passed on through the gate into the city, and Jesus rode up Mount Moriah, where the temple stood. And as he went, the people before and behind cried out aloud, "Hosanna to the Son of David." And the people in the city were stirred with the excitement. They came hurrying into the streets to ask, "What is the meaning of all this? "Who is this king you are bringing?" And the multitude answered, "This is Jesus, the prophet of Nazareth, of Galilee."

Then Jesus entered the temple and looked about upon the things there. Taking his disciples, he returned to Bethany to spend the night in the house of his friends.

Matt. 21:12–46; Mark 11:12–12:12;
Luke 19:41–20:19

Early in the morning Jesus and his disciples started away from Bethany to go again to the temple in Jerusalem. As they went, Jesus became hungry, and seeing a fig tree by the roadside he stopped to eat of its fruit. But there were no figs on the tree, only leaves, and Jesus turned away disappointed. As he walked away he said, "Never again shall man eat fruit from this tree."

When Jesus came to the temple he saw men in there who were buying and selling animals for sacrifice-offerings, and others who were called money-changers. Once before he had driven such men out of the temple, and now he drove them out the second time, saying, "In the Scriptures it is written, 'My house shall be called a house of prayer', but you have made it a den of thieves." For these men demanded more money for their sacrifice-offerings than they should have asked.

The wave of excitement was still running high in the city, and every one was eager to see Jesus. The blind and the lame came to him in the temple, and he healed them there. And little children came singing, "Hosanna to the Son of David!" No doubt they had heard the glad songs of the grown people who had come with Jesus from the Mount of Olives, and they, too, wished to praise this great man, who took little ones in his arms and blessed them.

The chief priests and scribes in the temple saw Jesus heal the blind and the lame, and they heard the children sing his praises. They were angered by these things, for they saw that every day the multitudes were becoming more excited about this Jesus. They came to him and asked, "Do you hear what these children are saying?" And Jesus replied, "Yes, I hear them. Have you never read these words in the Scriptures, 'Out of the mouths of little children thou hast perfected praise'?"

In the evening Jesus returned again with his disciples to Bethany, to be with his dear friends, and in the morning he went back to teach the eager people who gathered early to hear him. As they passed along the road by the fig tree that he had found only leaves on, the disciples saw that the tree had withered and now stood dry and dead. They were surprised that it should have changed so soon, and they spoke about it. Then Jesus taught them a lesson from the fig tree.

He said, "Have faith in God. If you have faith to believe that God hears you when you pray you shall do greater things than I have done by my words to this fig tree. For if you ask anything of God in prayer, and believe in your hearts that he hears you, the thing for which you ask shall be given."

When they came to the temple many people had already gathered to hear Jesus teach. The chief priests and the scribes were there also, ready to ask him a question, for they were not willing that he should teach the people. They demanded of him, "By what authority do you teach and work miracles? Who gave you this authority?"

Jesus knew how to answer them by asking a question of them. He said, "Was the baptism of John from heaven or of men? Tell me this and I will answer your question." Now the enemies of Jesus did not know how to answer. They had not received John's baptism as of God, and they feared to tell Jesus because many people were listening, and the people all claimed that surely John was a prophet of God. If they should not own John as a prophet they feared that the people would turn bitterly against them. Yet if they should say that John's baptism was of God they knew Jesus would ask why they had not believed him. So they said, "We cannot tell whether John's baptism was from heaven or of men." Then Jesus answered, "Neither will I tell you by what authority I do these things, or who gave this authority to me."

Again Jesus began to teach by story-sermons, called parables. He told them about a man who had two sons. This man called his elder son to him and said, "Son, go and work today in my vineyard." The boy answered his father roughly, saying, "I will not go!" But afterward he became sorry, and repented of his unwillingness to obey his father's command. Then he went to the vineyard and worked. To the second son the father spoke the same words of command, and this boy replied politely, "I go, sir." But he did not go. "Now," asked Jesus, "which of the two boys obeyed his father?" and the people answered, "The first."

Jesus said the two boys were like the two classes—the people whom the Pharisees and such called sinners, and the Pharisees and other leaders themselves. All these leaders claimed to be obedient, and yet they were not doing the things God had commanded, while the other people whom they called sinners had listened gladly to John's words and had been baptized by him.

Another story that Jesus told was about a man who planted a vineyard, and built a hedge about it, dug a winepress in it, and built a watchtower. Then he hired some men to care for it, and went away to another country. When the time came that the fruit of the vineyard should be ripened, he sent servants to get some of the fruit and bring it back to him. But the keepers of the vineyard treated the servants roughly. The first one who came they beat, and sent him away without any fruit. The second one they threw stones at and wounded him in the head. The third one they killed. Later other servants were sent, but the wicked keepers of the vineyard treated them all shamefully.

The owner of the vineyard was very sad, and he decided at last to send his own son. "They will know he is my son," he reasoned, "and they will respect him." But when the keepers looked out from the watchtower and saw the son coming, they said to each other, "The owner has sent his son. This vineyard will belong to him, because he is the heir, let us kill him, and take the vineyard for our own possession." So they caught him, and killed him, and threw his body outside the vineyard. "When the owner of that vineyard comes what will he do to those men?" asked Jesus. And the people answered, "He will cause them to be miserably destroyed, and he will give his vineyard into the care of better men who will give him some of its fruits."

Then Jesus looked boldly upon his enemies standing near and said, "The kingdom of God shall be taken from you, and shall be given to another nation, which will bring forth fruit." The chief priests and scribes knew he had spoken the parables against them, and they were angry. But they were afraid to seize him because they knew all the people standing round believed that Jesus was a great prophet.

Matt. 22:1–24:1; Mark 12:13–13:1;
Luke 20:20–21:4; John 12:20–36

While Jesus was teaching in the temple he told the people a parable that the kingdom of heaven is like a king who made a feast at the marriage of his son. The king prepared a great feast and invited guests from a city nearby. When everything was ready, the guests failed to come. He sent servants to remind them of their invitation to the wedding feast, still they would not come. They made fun of it, and went on about their own work. Some of them even treated the king's messengers cruelly and killed them.

The king heard about the conduct of those people, and

he was much displeased. He called out his army and sent his soldiers to destroy them and to burn their city. Then he invited other guests to the marriage feast, and the place was filled, for every one came who was bidden this time.

Among these guests were the poor and the rich, and the good and the bad, and the king furnished each one with a garment to wear. He wished to have them appear well in his presence. When all had arrived and put on their clean garments, he came in to see them and give them a welcome to the feast.

One man was present who refused to put on the clean garment that the king had provided for him. There he stood among all the others, clothed in his dirty rags. The king saw him and said, "Friend, why did you come in here without putting on the clean garment that I had provided for you to wear?" And the man hung his head, for he had no excuse to offer. The king was displeased with him because he had disobeyed orders, so he commanded his servants to seize the man, bind him hand and foot, and take him away to a dark place where he should be punished.

The Pharisees and other enemies of Jesus knew these parables were showing the people how they, the Pharisees and the other enemies, had refused to obey God, and they determined to put a stop to his teaching. They decided to ask questions of him, and prevent him from teaching in this way. So they sent some men who pretended to be good, and told these men to ask him whether it was wrong or right to pay the tribute money, or tax money, which Caesar, the Roman ruler, demanded of them.

The Jews disliked to pay this money, and Jesus' enemies

knew that if he should say it was right for them to pay the tax then the people would no longer care to make him their king. They would no longer follow him so eagerly and listen to his words, for they hated the Roman government. But if Jesus should say it was wrong to pay this tax money, then his enemies planned to tell the Roman officers that Jesus was unwilling to obey the Roman government, and they knew Jesus would be punished.

So the men came to Jesus and said, "Master, we know you are true, and that you teach the way of God in truth without caring whether men will be pleased with your teaching or not." Thus they flattered him, thinking he would be delighted to hear such favorable things said of himself. Then they continued: "Tell us just what you think, Is it right or wrong to pay this tribute money which Caesar demands of us Jews?" They thought Jesus would answer either yes or no. But they were mistaken.

Jesus could see the hearts of these evil men who were questioning him. He paid no attention to their flattering words, but said, "Why do you tempt me, you hypocrites? Show me the tribute money." And they brought him a penny. Jesus looked at the coin on both sides, then asked of them, "Whose image is this on the one side? and whose name is written here?" On one side of the coin was a picture of Caesar's head, and his name was written above it. The men replied that the image and the name on the coin were both Caesar's. "Then," said Jesus, "give to Caesar the things that belong to him, and give to God the things that belong to God."

This answer greatly surprised the men, for they had

thought they surely would catch Jesus in a trap where he would need to say yes or no. But he had replied so wisely they could not accuse him to any man.

Others came to question Jesus, and among them was a lawyer who asked, "Which is the greatest commandment of the law?" Jesus replied that the greatest commandment of the law was, "Thou shalt love the Lord thy God with all thy heart, and with all thy soul, and with all thy mind, and with all thy strength: This is the first commandment. And the second greatest is this: Thou shalt love thy neighbor as much as thyself. No other commandments are so important as these two." The lawyer answered, "You have spoken well, for to love the Lord God in this way and to love one's neighbor as much as one's own self is surely more pleasing to God than burnt offerings and sacrifices."

Jesus was pleased with this reply of the lawyer. He saw that the lawyer understood the meaning of God's Word better than did many who pretended to be teachers of it. And he told the lawyer that he was near to the kingdom of God.

While Jesus was in the temple, some men came to Philip, one of the twelve disciples, and asked permission to see Jesus. These men were Gentiles, they were Greeks by birth, and they had come to worship the God of the Jews, so they were called proselytes. Because they were Gentiles they could not enter the part of the temple where Jesus sat teaching the people who thronged him there. They could come no farther than the outside court, called the court of the Gentiles. But they had heard much about this wonderful teacher from Galilee, and they wished to see him. Philip told Andrew, another disciple, and together they hurried to tell

Jesus that strangers from Greece, a country far away, were waiting in the court of the Gentiles to catch a glimpse of him.

When Jesus heard about the inquirers from distant Greece he said to Philip and Andrew, "The hour is come that the Son of man should be glorified." He spoke to them about his coming death for the sins of the people, but the disciples could not understand his words. And because Jesus could feel pain just as we do he shrank from the thought of dying on the cross. He felt troubled because the time was drawing so near when he should die. And he said, prayerfully, "Father, save me from this hour." Then he remembered that his life-work would not be finished if he did not die for lost sinners, so he added, "Father, glorify thy name." And a voice spoke from heaven, "I have glorified it, and will glorify it again." The people standing by heard the voice but could not understand the words that were spoken. Some thought the voice sounded like thunder; others said, "An angel spoke to him." But Jesus said the voice had spoken to prove to them that God had heard him.

After teaching, Jesus had sat down near a place in the temple called the treasury. Here were money boxes in which the people's offerings were received. And Jesus saw the rich pass by the boxes and throw in large offerings. Finally he saw a poor widow come into the treasury and stop beside a box to throw in her small offering of only two little coins. Together these coins were worth less than a penny. But Jesus told his disciples that the poor widow had given more than the rich people, for they had given out of full purses whereas she had emptied the last of her money into the box. He wished to teach them that God looks at the heart of the giver, for God saw that the poor widow gave her all because she loved him, whereas the rich people gave their offerings because it was their duty to give.

Then Jesus and his disciples left the temple, and went out to the Mount of Olives. Never again did Jesus walk in the courts of the Lord's house on Mount Moriah, for soon afterward his enemies took him and did to him all they had wished to do.

Matt. 23:37–25:46; Mark 13;
Luke 21:5–38

As Jesus left the temple for the last time, his disciples spoke to him about the beauty of the Lord's house. Like all other Jews, they took much pride in the temple where God was worshiped. And they were surprised to hear Jesus say, "The time is coming when the stones of these buildings shall be torn apart."

On the Mount of Olives, Jesus rested for a while before going on to Bethany. And his disciples gathered around him there to ask when the time should come that the beautiful temple would be destroyed. No one else was near to disturb them, and Jesus talked long and earnestly to his disciples about the things that would happen to Jerusalem, and later to the whole world. He told them that men would come who would claim to be the Christ of God, and that many would believe in them. He said that great wars would be fought among the nations of the earth, and that troubles of different kinds would come upon the people. Then he said that before the end of time the gospel of the kingdom would be preached, not only among the Jews, but to all people in every part of the world. How strange these things must have sounded to the disciples, for they had always believed that salvation belonged to the Jews only.

Then Jesus told the disciples the parable of the ten young women, called virgins. Five of these young women were wise and five were foolish. All had been invited to the marriage of a friend, and they started to meet the wedding-party. They took their lamps with them to give light, for the wedding would take place at night and only those carrying lights would be allowed to join the wedding party.

But the wedding party was slow in coming, and the young women grew tired waiting. So they fell asleep. At midnight a cry was made that the wedding party was coming, and the young women aroused and began at once to trim their lamps to be ready to join the procession when it came by.

Now the five who were wise poured more oil into their lamps; for they saw the light was growing dim, and they had brought an extra supply of oil with them. But the five who were foolish had brought no more oil, and they, too, saw that their lights were growing dim. "What shall we do?" they asked each other. Then they spoke to their wise friends and said, "Please give some of your oil to us, for our lights are going out!"

The wise young women did not have enough to give to their friends in distress, so they answered, "You must go to them who sell and buy for yourselves. We do not have enough to share." And while they hurried away to buy more oil, the wedding party came, and the five wise young women joined the party and went to the home where the marriage festivities would take place.

When all the guests had entered, the door was shut, and no other persons could enter. The foolish young women came after the door had been shut, and they knocked; but the bridegroom would not let them in. They had come too late.

By this story Jesus wished to teach his disciples to watch and be ready, for they should not know the time when he would call for them to leave this world and go to be with him. If they should not be ready when he should call, they would have no time left in which to make ready, but, like the foolish young women, they would be shut out of heaven.

Jesus told the disciples what will happen at the end of the world. He said that then the Son of man will come in his glory, bringing all the angels with him. And he will sit upon the throne of his glory. And before him all nations of the earth shall be gathered, and he will divide the good from the evil. Those who have believed in him he will place on his right, and those who have disobeyed he will place on his left, just as a shepherd in that country divided his sheep from his goats. The disciples no doubt had watched the shepherds come in from the fields and separate the sheep from the goats in their great flocks, and they understood how this separation will be.

"Then shall the Son of man be King," said Jesus, "and he will say to them on his right, 'Come, you who are blessed of my Father, and dwell in the kingdom which has been prepared for you. For I was hungry, and you fed me; I was thirsty and you gave me drink; I was a stranger, and you gave me shelter; I was shivering with cold, and you gave me clothes to keep me warm; I was sick, and you visited me; I was in prison, and you came to see me even there.' And the ones on his right will reply, 'Lord, when did we see you in need and help you thus?' And the King will answer, 'Whenever you helped one of my needy brothers, even the least of them, you helped me.'

"Then the King will turn to those on his left, and will say to them, 'Depart from me, you who are cursed, and go away into everlasting fire, which has been made ready for the devil and his evil spirits. For I was hungry, and you did not feed me; I was thirsty, and you gave me no water; I was a stranger, and you gave me no shelter; without clothes, and you did not give clothes to me; sick, and you did not visit me; in prison, and you did not come to me there.' And the ones on his left will reply, 'Lord, when did we see you hungry, or thirsty, or without clothes, or a stranger, or sick, or in prison, and not help you?' And he will say to them, 'Whenever you refused to help one of my brothers, even the poorest of them, you refused to help me.'

"And those on the right," said Jesus, "will go into life eternal in heaven, while those on the left shall be turned away into everlasting torment."

THE DEATH AND RESURRECTION OF JESUS

Matt. 26:17–30; Mark 14:12–26;
Luke 22:3–39; John 13

Two disciples, Peter and John, were hurrying along the road from Bethany to Jerusalem. They were going on an errand for their master. The day had come when the lamb for the Passover Feast should be killed, and Jesus had chosen these two disciples to go to Jerusalem and prepare the feast that the Twelve should eat with him that evening.

After they had passed through the city gate, they looked about to find a man carrying a pitcher of water. Men seldom carried water pitchers in the streets, for such work was usually left for women to do. But Jesus had told them they would see a man carrying a water pitcher, and they did. Jesus also told them to follow the man to the house where he should go with his pitcher, so they followed.

At the house they met the owner, and to him they gave the message that Jesus had sent. This was the message: "Our master sent us to ask your permission for him to use your guest room in which to eat the Passover supper with his disciples." And the owner of the house led them to a nice room upstairs which was furnished with a table and couches on which the guests might recline while they ate. No doubt this owner knew Jesus, and was glad to give him the use of the guest room in his home.

When evening came, Jesus and the other ten joined Peter and John and together they sat around the table in that quiet room upstairs. A feeling of sadness crept into the hearts of the disciples, for their Master spoke to them so earnestly about going away soon.

It was so hard for these men to believe that Jesus would really be taken away from them. They had seen him do such wonderful things that it seemed impossible to think men could ever kill him. And soon they were talking about other matters at the supper table. Some were wondering who would be the greatest in the kingdom that they expected Jesus to set up soon.

Jesus knew their thoughts, and he wished to teach them more about the kind of kingdom he was bringing to mankind. He rose up suddenly from the table, laid aside his outer garment, and tied a towel about his waist. Then he took a basin of water and began to wash the disciples' feet.

The disciples looked at each other in silent astonishment. They could not understand why he should be doing this humble act of service, for they had washed the dust from their feet before coming into that upper room. Finally Jesus came to Peter with his basin. But that disciple pulled his feet away, and exclaimed, "Lord, you shall never wash my feet!" "Then," answered Jesus calmly, "you shall never have a part in my kingdom." At this Peter changed his mind and he said, "Lord, you may wash my feet, and even my hands and my head." Very desirous was this disciple of having a part in Jesus' kingdom. But by washing their feet, Jesus did not mean in this way to prepare the hearts of his disciples for his work. He said to them, "You are clean already, but not all." For he knew which one was not a true disciple.

When the strange washing was over, Jesus laid aside the towel and took up his garment again. Then he returned to his place at the table, beside John, and began to explain to his disciples what he had just done to them: "You call me Lord, and Master," said he, "and so I am. If I, your Lord and Master, have washed your feet, you ought to wash one another's feet. For I have given you an example that you should do to each other as I have done to you. The servant is not greater than his master, and if you would be good servants you will obey my words. If you know my commands, you will be happy when you obey them."

Jesus also said that one of them should give him into the hands of his enemies, who would take his life. This seemed hard to believe, but the disciples knew Jesus' words of prophecy always came true, so they were amazed. Instead of looking at each other accusingly, each man thought of himself. And each one said, "Lord, is it I?"

John, the disciple who liked to be near Jesus, was sitting next to his master at the supper. Peter motioned to John and whispered, "Ask which one will do this dreadful deed." So John asked Jesus, and Jesus replied in low tones, "The one to whom I shall give a piece of bread when I have dipped it in the dish." John watched carefully, and soon he saw Jesus give a piece of bread to Judas Iscariot.

After Judas had taken the bread that Jesus gave to him, Jesus said, "That thou doest, do quickly." Then the desire in his heart to get rid of this master became stronger, and Judas hurried out of the room into the gloom of night. None of the disciples understood what Jesus meant, but they supposed because Judas carried the money bag that he was going to do something for their master.

Jesus then, after supper, took bread and blessed it and broke it in pieces, giving parts to each of the disciples, and saying, "Take this bread and eat it, for it is my body, which is broken for you." Then he took the cup and when he had given thanks he passed it to them, saying, "Drink this, for it is my blood, which is shed for you, for I will never again drink of the fruit of the vine with you until that day when I drink it new in the kingdom of God."

They lingered a while longer in the upper room, and Jesus talked earnestly to them about the time when he should go away and leave them alone. He urged them to remember his commandment to love each other as he had loved them, and he told them that he would prepare a place for them in his Father's house.

Peter insisted that he would not leave Jesus, but would go with him wherever he went. Jesus told him that he could not go now, but that he might come later on. He also told Peter that, bold as he believed himself to be, he would prove himself a coward before daylight should return, for he would forsake Jesus and even deny that he had ever known him. Thus the Lord's Supper had been instituted. Then Jesus and his disciples sang a hymn together, and quietly left the upper room, going out of Jerusalem into a garden nearby.

Matt. 26:36–75; Mark 14:32–72;
Luke 22:39–71; John 18:1–27

Through the deep shadows that fell from the buildings along the streets a silent figure glided along, hurrying toward the assembly room where the enemies of Jesus were sitting together waiting. That silent figure was the evil-minded disciple, Judas Iscariot, who was hurrying on his way to sell his Lord.

Soon the footsteps of Judas fell on the floor of the hall, and his knock sounded on the door of the assembly room. In reply to the call, "Who is there?" came the answer, "He for whom you wait," and quickly the door was thrown open and Judas entered. Now there followed a hasty conversation, some argument, and finally thirty pieces of silver were counted out and handed to Judas. Then the assembly broke up, each man hurrying to get a torch or to summon the soldiers who should go on their midnight errand.

While this was taking place, Jesus and the eleven disciples had left the room upstairs where they had eaten the last Passover supper together, and had gone outside the city to a garden across the brook Kidron. Here at the entrance of the garden Jesus had told eight of the disciples to wait, and, taking with him Peter, James, and John, he had gone into the deeper shadows of the trees to pray.

But while Jesus prayed the disciples fell asleep. They could not understand why he should seem so troubled and they did not know how to comfort him. They allowed their own sleepy feelings to overcome their love for him, and just when he longed to have them near to pray with him they slept. Three times Jesus went to waken Peter, James, and John, but not once did they offer him the comfort he sought. Then while he prayed in agony alone God sent an angel from heaven to strengthen and comfort him. For Jesus knew the sorrow that was soon to come; he knew what Judas was even then doing; and he knew his enemies would not cease to torture him till he should be hanging dead upon the cross. Not only that, for Jesus knew also that he must bear the sins of the whole world in order to become the Savior of men. And because he had a body such as we have, he dreaded to suffer the pain of such a death, and he dreaded to be left alone by those whom he loved. So he asked God to take away the suffering from him if such a thing should be possible. But he added, "Let thy will, not mine, be done."

When Jesus had roused the sleepy disciples the third time, he told them to arise; for it was time for them to be going on their way. And they rose up to follow him out of the garden. But as they went toward the entrance they saw a band of men coming to them carrying torches as if they were searching for some one. Jesus walked up to the men and asked, "For whom are you seeking?" and they replied, "For Jesus of Nazareth."

"I am he," answered Jesus. And the men fell backward. When they rose, Jesus asked them the second time whom they were seeking, and again they said, "For Jesus of Nazareth." Judas, the unfaithful disciple, was with the band of men, and he stepped forward and cried, "Hail, Master!" and kissed Jesus on the cheek. But Jesus knew the evil thought that was in Judas mind, and he looked sadly into the guilty face of his unfaithful disciple and asked, "Judas, do you betray the Son of man with a kiss?"

Judas had told the band of men the sign by which they might know whom to take for their prisoner, and that sign was the kiss he had given to Jesus. Now the soldiers took hold of Jesus roughly and prepared to lead him away.

At this Peter was thoroughly aroused from his sleep. Drawing a short sword, which he carried in his belt, he struck at one of the soldiers and cut off his ear. But Jesus seemed displeased, and told Peter to put away his sword. Then he healed the soldier's ear; and Peter, unable to understand how he might now defend his master, sank back into the shadows with the other frightened disciples.

The soldiers then bound their prisoner, and the procession started toward the assembly room where the enemies of Jesus were waiting impatiently. And far behind Peter followed, wondering what he should do, and yet fearing that the soldiers might take him, also.

First the soldiers brought Jesus to the house of a man named Annas, who was father-in-law of the high priest, Caiaphas, and here his trial began. John, one of the disciples, gained admittance at the door, for he was acquainted with the household of the high priest. And he went in where Jesus was. But Peter stood outside, for he was a stranger, and the doorkeeper, a young girl, would not let him in.

Presently John spoke to the doorkeeper, and she allowed him to take Peter into the courtroom, for the night was cold. When Peter was inside the young girl said, "Are you not also one of his disciples?" But Peter was afraid, and he said, "No, I did not know the man."

In the open court a fire was burning, and Peter went near to warm himself. Around the fire stood other men, some who were servants in the high priest's house and others who were officers.

One of the men by the fire then turned to Peter and asked, "Are you not one of this man's disciples?" Again fear crept into Peter's heart, and he replied stoutly, "No, I am not!" But a soldier standing by who had been in the garden when Jesus was taken had seen Peter use his sword, and he spoke, saying, "I saw you in the garden with him!" Peter denied fiercely, and pretended that he had never known Jesus at all.

While this had been happening to Peter, out in the high priest's courtyard, the high priest and others had been asking Jesus questions about his teachings and had been treating him shamefully. Then the enemies of Jesus led their prisoner out of the high priest's house, and as he passed by he looked sadly upon Peter. And Peter remembered how Jesus had told him that before the return of another day he would deny three times that he had ever known the Lord. Now tears filled Peter's eyes, and he turned blindly away from the fire and rushed out of the door, to weep bitterly. He saw himself no longer a true man, brave, and ready to help in the work of his master, but a coward, ashamed to own that he had once proudly followed the innocent man who now stood bound in chains and condemned to die.

Matt. 27:1–54; Mark 15:1–39;
Luke 23:1–47; John 18:28–19:31

After the sad, long night when Jesus was captured in the garden, morning came at last, and the news began to spread through the city streets that Jesus, the prophet from Galilee, was now a prisoner. His friends were terrified, while his enemies laughed in wicked glee. And the soldiers led him before the Roman governor, Pilate, for this governor now took the place of the King Herod who had tried to kill Jesus when he was born, in Bethlehem.

Pilate knew nothing about Jesus. He took him into his judgment hall and talked a while with him. And he was surprised to hear the wisdom of this one who was condemned to die. He went out to them and said, "I find no fault in this man." But the enemies of Jesus cried the more loudly that he should be put to death, saying that he had stirred up the people throughout the country, even from Galilee.

When Pilate heard that Jesus was from Galilee, he said, "This man belongs to the country that Herod rules." This Herod was a son of the wicked king who tried to take Jesus' life when he was a baby. Pilate sent Jesus to Herod at once, for Herod was in Jerusalem at that time.

Now this same Herod had caused John the Baptist to be put to death. He had heard much about Jesus, but he had never seen this prophet from Galilee. When the soldiers came, bringing Jesus bound with chains, Herod was glad, for he hoped that Jesus might do some miracle before him. At once he began to ask questions of Jesus, but not one question would Jesus answer. The chief priests and the scribes stood round about and said all kinds of evil things about Jesus, still he would not speak one word to defend himself.

Finally Herod grew impatient with this silent prisoner. A wicked thought came into his heart, so he began to make fun of Jesus. With his soldiers he mocked Jesus, dressing him in rich garments and pretending to honor him as a king. Then he sent him back to Pilate.

Now Pilate's wife had heard about the trial of Jesus and she was greatly troubled, for that night she had dreamed about him. She sent a message to her husband, urging him to set Jesus free, saying, "He is a just man, not worthy of death." Pilate, too, wished to free Jesus; for he could find no guilt in him. He told the accusers that neither he nor Herod had been able to find him guilty of death. But the mob now cried, "If you set this man free you are not a friend of Caesar, and Caesar will dismiss you from being our governor." Pilate knew the people could accuse him to Caesar if they were displeased with him, and being a coward he chose rather to let an innocent man suffer than to be in danger of losing his position as governor.

As the trial went on, Judas Iscariot saw that Jesus was condemned to die. Now his guilty conscience troubled him greatly. He had hoped that Jesus would free himself in some miraculous way from the power of his enemies; but now he saw that Jesus was allowing himself to be helpless in their hands. The money that he had taken from the enemies of Jesus seemed to burn his flesh, so he hurried back to the chief priests and scribes, saying, "I have sold an innocent man! I have sinned!"

The chief priests and scribes looked scornfully upon Judas and replied, "What is that to us? You yourself must answer for your sin." And they turned away from him, refusing to take back the money they had given him for doing the dreadful act. Neither would Judas keep the money, so he threw it upon the floor of the temple and ran down the long flight of steps, away to a lonely place, where he hung himself and died.

Before giving Jesus up to die, Pilate talked to the restless mob about another prisoner whom he held—a wicked man named Barabbas, who as a robber had caused much trouble to the Jews. At the time of the Feast it was customary to release a prisoner, and Pilate asked whether he should release Barabbas, the wicked robber whom the people feared, or Jesus, the innocent man whom they hated. And with loud cries the people answered, "Set Barabbas free!" Then Pilate asked, "What shall I do with Jesus?" and they answered, "Crucify him! Crucify him!"

So the trial came to an end, and Pilate called some Roman soldiers and told them to lead Jesus away to be crucified. First he took water in a basin and washed his hands before the people, saying, "I am not guilty of the death of this innocent man." The people cried out, "We ourselves will bear the blame; let his blood be on our heads!"

The Roman soldiers took Jesus and put a crown of thorns upon his head. Then they put a reed in his hand, and, bowing before him mockingly called him the king of the Jews. They also blindfolded his eyes, and spat upon him, and struck him with their hands, saying, "Tell us, prophet, who is it who struck you?" All these shameful things Jesus bore in silence for he was suffering in the place of those who deserved to suffer for their own sins. Finally the soldiers took off the purple robe and dressed him once more in his own clothes. Then they led him away outside the city to nail him on a cross. They took two other prisoners, men who had been thieves, and laid heavy crosses on the bared backs of these men, then led them away with Jesus to die.

A crowd of curious people followed the soldiers through the gate to the hillside where the crucifixion took place. Many in the crowd were enemies of Jesus, others were friends who longed to help but could not. As they went, Jesus sank down beneath the weight of the heavy cross he bore, and could not rise again. The cruel soldiers then called a stranger from the crowd and placed the cross upon his shoulder, for Jesus was too weak to carry it any farther.

On the hillside of Calvary the crowd stopped, and the soldiers began to strip their prisoners of their clothing and to fasten their hands and their feet to the crosses. Then they raised the crosses high in the air and planted them securely in the ground, leaving the prisoners there until death should relieve them of their misery. Jesus prayed when they were crucifying him and said, "Father, forgive them, for they know not what they do."

The cross on which Jesus was crucified stood between the two crosses on which the thieves were hung, and a writing was nailed above the head of Jesus, which said in three languages, "This is Jesus, the King of the Jews." When Jesus' enemies read the writing they were much displeased and hurried to ask Pilate to change it, that it might read thus: "He called himself the King of the Jews." But Pilate would not change the writing, and all who passed by could read what he had written, though they were strangers in Judah.

While Jesus hung on the cross, one of the thieves began to mock him, but the other begged to be forgiven and to be remembered when Jesus came into his kingdom. He believed that Jesus was really the King from heaven, which the Jews were unwilling to receive. And Jesus saw his faith, and said to him, "Today you shall be with me in paradise." Then the thief knew that his sins were forgiven, and though he was suffering much pain a glad joy came into his heart.

While Jesus hung on the cross he saw a group of sorrowing friends standing at the edge of the crowd, and among them was his own mother. John, the disciple who loved him so much, was also there, and Jesus asked John to take care of his mother from that time.

The enemies of Jesus stood around the cross, making fun of him and telling him to come down if he were the Son of God. Even the chief priests and the scribes were there, and they said, "He said he could save others, but he cannot save himself! If he is the king of Israel, let him come down, and we will believe in him, too."

About noonday the sky suddenly grew dark. For three hours the great darkness lasted, then Jesus cried with a loud voice, saying, "It is finished!" and soon he died. The Roman captain who stood near the cross, and the soldiers who were with him, saw the rocks torn apart by a terrible earthquake that came, and they were frightened. And the captain said to his soldiers, "Truly this man was the Son of God!"

Matt. 27:55–28:1; Mark 15:42–16:5;
Luke 23:50–24:1; John 19:31–20:1

The people who had been so gleeful when Jesus was taken prisoner and crucified still felt troubled about him. They could not put the thoughts of him out of their minds. The next day would be their Sabbath, and they did not wish to have him hanging on the cross, with the words, "This is the King of the Jews," written above his head.

However, a rich man named Joseph, who was also a ruler among the Jews, now came boldly into Pilate's judgment hall and asked permission to take the body of Jesus and bury it. This man, although a ruler, had loved Jesus and he had taken no part in the wicked plots of his fellow rulers. He with Nicodemus, the Pharisee, had long believed in Jesus, but for fear of his enemies these two men had not made known their belief. Now with Pilate's permission they went to Calvary. They took Jesus' body and wrapped it in rich linen clothes with the sweet spices and perfumes that Nicodemus the Pharisee had brought. Then they laid it in a new grave, or tomb, which had been cut out of a large rock. This grave opened into a garden, and Joseph had intended it for his own burial place when he should die. Some of the women who had often been with Jesus when he taught the multitudes, stood by watching when Joseph and Nicodemus laid the body of their beloved friend in the dark tomb, and they saw the men roll a heavy stone before the door.

Evening had now come and the Jews' Sabbath had commenced, for their Sabbath began at sunset on Friday evening and ended at sunset on Saturday evening. The sorrowing friends of Jesus therefore hastily returned to their homes to keep the Sabbath in the quiet manner that the Jews had been taught to keep it.

But the enemies of Jesus began to fear that Jesus' grave might be disturbed by his friends. They remembered that Jesus had said he would rise on the third day, and they said to each other, "His disciples may come to steal him away and then declare that he has risen. Then perhaps more people will believe in him and we shall be despised by them." So they hurried to Pilate and told him about their fears, and asked permission to place his Roman seal upon the stone in front of Jesus' grave. They also wanted Pilate to command soldiers to guard the tomb, so that no one should come by night and break the seal and take away the body. And Pilate allowed them to place his seal upon the great stone and to station soldiers to guard the grave by day and by night.

The women who had watched Joseph and Nicodemus lay the body of Jesus away longed to show their love for Jesus, and after sunset on the next day they hurriedly prepared some sweet perfumes. Then they planned to go early the next morning to anoint the body of their dear friend, even though he had been buried.

But the eleven disciples, stricken with sorrow, hid themselves from the scornful glances of passers-by. They had forgotten the words of Jesus, that he would rise again on the third day. The cruel act of Judas, one of their own number, and the defenseless attitude of their master when in the hands of his enemies had so disappointed them that they bowed their heads in anguish and grief. Nothing seemed left for them now, when their glorious hopes of the kingdom of heaven had disappeared like a broken bubble. And they mourned and wept tears of disappointment, while a fear of the Jews' further displeasure only added to their weight of grief.

Early on the morning of the third day, before the sun had risen, a group of sorrowing women crept out of the city and sped along the highway toward the garden tomb. As they went they wondered who would roll away the stone from the door of the grave, that they might go inside and pour their sweet perfumes upon the body of Jesus. But when they came near they saw the stone was rolled away and that the tomb was empty. Other visitors had come to the tomb even earlier than they. And the body of Jesus was not there.

Matt. 28:2–16; Mark 16:5–14;
Luke 24:4–12; John 20:2–18

The hours of watching dragged slowly by to the Roman soldiers who guarded the tomb where the body of Jesus lay. No one had come even to visit the grave, and perhaps the soldiers laughed at the fears of the Jews.

The eastern sky was beginning to light up with the promise of a new day when suddenly the ground beneath the watcher's feet began to tremble. Another earthquake had come. Then the fearful watchers saw a mighty angel come down from the sky and roll the stone away from the door of the tomb and sit upon it. The face of this angel had the appearance of lightning, and the garments he wore were as white as snow. At sight of him the soldiers fell to the ground, trembling and helpless, and lay there as if they were dead. All this happened because Jesus had, in the grave, come back to life. He was risen from the dead.

When the women came to the garden they found the tomb empty, and the angel had not yet gone back to heaven. At first the women did not see the angel, and they wondered who had come and stolen the body of their Lord. Mary Magdalene left the others and ran quickly to tell Peter and John that the body of Jesus had been taken away from the tomb and hidden they knew not where.

After Mary had gone from them, the other women saw in the empty tomb the beautiful angel, and they were afraid and bowed themselves to the ground. But the angel said, "Do not be afraid. Why are you seeking the living among the dead? Jesus is not here; he is risen as he said. Go quickly and tell his disciples and Peter that he is alive and will meet them in Galilee."

The women ran from the place, filled with joy yet trembling with excitement and fear. The good news that the angel told seemed too wonderful to be true, still they believed and hurried to tell the disciples and other friends who were sorrowing.

But the disciples refused to believe the glad message. Peter and John ran to see the empty tomb for themselves, and when they came to the place they found no one, for the soldiers had risen and fled into the city to tell their strange experience to the enemies of Jesus who had stationed them to watch by the grave. John outran Peter, and coming first to the grave he looked and saw it was empty. Then Peter came, and he went into the dark room where the body of Jesus had lain. He saw there the grave clothes that Joseph had wrapped round the body of Jesus, and he believed that surely Jesus was alive once more. John, too, entered the grave and saw the clothes lying where Jesus had left them, and he also believed.

Mary Magdalene had not stayed in the garden long enough to hear the message of the angel, and now she returned from the city, longing to find the place where her crucified Lord had been taken. She did not yet know of the new hopes that were gladdening the hearts of her friends. Entering the garden again, she stood by the empty grave and wept. Then she stooped down and looked into the grave and saw two angels sitting, one at the head and another at the foot of where the body of Jesus had lain. They said to her, "Woman, why are you weeping?" and she replied, "Because they have taken away my Lord and I do not know where they have laid him." Then turning about she saw Jesus himself standing near. But tears blinded her eyes, and she did nor know him. He, too, asked her why she wept, and supposing him to be the man who cared for the garden, she said, "Sir, if you have carried away my Lord, tell me where you have laid him that I may take him." Then Jesus said, "Mary!" and she knew his voice.

What glad joy filled Mary's heart when she knew that Jesus was speaking to her again. She fell at his feet and cried, "Master!" Then he told her to go at once and tell her sorrowing friends that she had seen him and that he had told her to tell them he was going to ascend to their heavenly Father's home.

While these things were happening, the soldiers came

into the city and told the chief priests what had taken place in the garden tomb. And the chief priests were alarmed. They quickly called the other enemies of Jesus, and they all wondered what to do. They had no thoughts of accepting Jesus even though he had truly risen from the dead. They still hoped to persuade the people that Jesus had been a false prophet, so they decided on a plan and they asked the soldiers to help them carry it out. They offered them much money if only they would promise to tell no one else that Jesus had risen and an angel had opened the tomb. They urged the soldiers to tell the people that the disciples came and stole Jesus' body away while they were lying asleep.

The Roman soldiers cared nothing about the Jews and their religion, and they gladly took the money and went away. And when they were questioned about the disappearance of Jesus' body from the grave they said the disciples had stolen it while they slept.

Luke 24:13–48; John 20:19–31

The Passover Feast had ended, and some of the visitors at Jerusalem were returning to their homes. Along the roadway leading from the city of Jerusalem to the village of Emmaus, seven miles distant, two men were walking slowly, with bowed heads. They were friends of Jesus, and they were troubled about the news that had come to the city just before they started on their journey.

As these men talked together about the trial and crucifixion of Jesus, and about the women's message that early morning, suddenly a stranger joined them and asked, "Why is it that you are so sad? "What are you talking about so earnestly?" The men replied, "Can it be possible that you have not heard about the sad things that have been happening during these few days past?" And the stranger asked, "What things?"

The men began to tell this stranger about Jesus of Nazareth whom they had hoped would deliver their nation from the rule of the Romans and set up a kingdom. They told him how the chief priests and rulers had become jealous of him because he was such a mighty prophet, and how they captured him and caused him to be crucified. They told him that Jesus had died on the cross and that his body had been buried by loving friends in a nice, new tomb. "And this is the third day since these things happened," they said, "and this morning some women of our company astonished us by saying they had gone early to the tomb and had seen that his body had been taken away. But they said angels were there, and the angels said he had risen from the dead. Then some of our own number hurried to the grave and found that it was indeed empty, but they did not see the angels nor did they see our risen Lord."

The stranger listened patiently, and when they had finished he began to talk to them about the teachings of Moses' law and of the prophets concerning the promised Redeemer of Israel. He showed them by the word of God's book that Jesus, the prophet of Galilee, should suffer these very things and rise again the third day if he would really be the Redeemer for whom they were longing. And the men listened silently, wondering who this stranger could be.

Presently they came near to the village of Emmaus, and the two men asked the stranger to stop with them until the next morning, as the day had nearly ended. So he stopped with them. And when they sat down to eat their evening meal he took bread, blessed it, and gave it to them, and they knew at once that he was Jesus, their risen Lord. But he disappeared from their sight.

Now the two men understood why the women who had seen the angels seemed so full of joy. They, too, believed in the risen Lord, and their hearts were filled with gladness. They rose up from the table and hurried back to Jerusalem to tell the disciples that they had seen the Lord.

The deep shades of night had fallen over Jerusalem when the men at last came to the house where the disciples and some of their friends were gathered together. When they entered the room they saw that a change had come over these people who had been so sad. Now every one seemed happy, and excited about something. "Jesus is indeed risen," they cried joyously, "for Peter has seen him!" Then the two men told how he had appeared to them on their way to Emmaus, and how they had not known him until he had blessed and broken bread at their evening meal.

While they talked together suddenly Jesus himself appeared in their midst. And they were frightened, for the doors were closed when he entered and they supposed he was a spirit. But he spoke to them and said, "Why are you fearful? See my hands and my feet; touch me, and see that I am not a spirit, for a spirit does not have flesh and bones as I have." Then he asked for something to eat, and they gave him a piece of fish and some honey, which he ate before them. Great was their joy on beholding him once more in their midst, after they had seen him so cruelly tortured and killed.

But Thomas, one of the disciples, was not present when Jesus appeared. And he would not believe when the others told him that they had seen the Lord. He said, "Except I see in his hands the print of the nails and put my fingers into the nail prints, and except I thrust my hand into the place where the spear cut his side, I will not believe."

A week passed by, and again the disciples were together in a room, the doors being closed, and this time Thomas was with them. Then Jesus appeared as suddenly as he had come before, and he said to them all, "Peace be to you!" While they were wondering at his strange coming he called Thomas and said, "Behold my hands, and put your finger into the print of the nails, and put your hand into the place where the spear cut my side. And do not doubt, but believe."

Now Thomas worshiped Jesus, saying, "My Lord, and my God!" To him Jesus said, "You believe because you have seen; but blessed are those who will believe though they do not see me."

Mark 16:15–19; Luke 24:50–53;
John 21; Acts 1:1–14

F ar up in Galilee, away from the reach of their enemies, a group of men and women met together on a mountainside and waited for the appearance of their Lord. And Jesus came to them there, and talked with them again as earnestly as he had talked in other days. And they rejoiced to see him once more and worshiped him, but some doubted that he was really the same Jesus who had been nailed to the cross.

One day after this meeting some of the disciples who had been fishermen returned to the Sea of Galilee. The familiar sight of the water and fishing boats floating about on the surface stirred within Peter's heart a desire to again go fishing. So he told his companions, and they said, "We will go with you."

All that night the men stayed in their ship, toiling with their net; but not one fish did they catch. When morning came they drew near to the shore and saw a stranger standing there beside a fire of coals. He called to them and asked whether they had any fish. They replied that they had caught none, and he bade them cast their net into the water once more, this time on the right side of the ship. They obeyed, and now the net was filled.

John, the disciple who often went with Peter and James, now whispered to his companions, "It is the Lord." And immediately Peter wrapped his fisher's coat about his body and jumped overboard to swim to shore, so eager was he to come to Jesus. The others remained in the ship and brought it to the landing. Then Jesus commanded them to bring some of the fish they had caught, and Peter drew the net from out of the water. In it they had taken one hundred and fifty-three large fishes, yet the net was not broken. Then Jesus asked the men to come and eat, for he had already prepared fish and bread on the burning coals.

After they had eaten, Jesus talked with Peter, the disciple who had denied him at the time of his trial. He asked Peter three times if he loved him, and each time Peter replied, "Yes, Lord, you know that I love you." Peter believed that Jesus knew all things, and he felt sad because Jesus asked him this same question the third time. Then he remembered how only a short while ago he had denied three times that he ever knew Jesus. Now he declared three times that he loved him, and Jesus told him to feed his lambs and sheep.

Peter had heard Jesus speak a parable one day about the Good Shepherd, who gave his life for his sheep. And he knew that Jesus had called himself the Good Shepherd. Now he understood that Jesus had died for the sins of the people, and he believed that men and women were the sheep whom Jesus meant that he should feed. Not their bodies, but their souls were hungry to be fed, and Jesus wanted Peter to leave his work as a fisherman and become a preacher of the gospel. In this way he could feed the people.

Then Jesus told Peter words like these: "When you were a young man you went wherever you wished, but when you shall become an old man you shall stretch out your hands and another shall carry you where you do not wish to go." By these words he meant that when Peter should grow old he would be put to death because he loved Jesus. Then he said to Peter, "Follow me."

Peter turned about and saw John standing by. At once he asked, "Lord, what shall this man do?" But Jesus said, "Never mind about John's work; see that you follow me."

Forty days passed by, and during these days Jesus often spoke with his disciples about the kingdom of God. Still they did not understand that it would not be an earthly kingdom, like the kingdom of David had been. At last the time came for their farewell meeting.

During this time Jesus appeared to his disciples and when they saw him, they worshiped him, but some doubted. And Jesus came and spake unto them, saying, "All power is given unto me in heaven and in earth. Go ye therefore, and teach all nations, baptizing them in the name of the Father, and of the Son, and of the Holy Ghost."

While they talked earnestly together, Jesus said, "John the Baptist baptized you with water, but you shall be baptized with the Holy Spirit in a few days." And some of the disciples asked, "Will you at that time restore the kingdom of Israel?" But Jesus said, "It is not for you to know the plans of the heavenly Father; but you shall receive power from heaven when the Holy Spirit comes upon you, and this power will cause you to witness boldly to me in Jerusalem, in all the country of Judah, in Samaria, and in the farthest parts of the world. But do not go away from Jerusalem until the Holy Spirit is given to you."

While Jesus talked to them they were standing together

on the Mount of Olives, and suddenly the disciples saw him being caught up into heaven. They watched until he disappeared from sight in bright clouds, after which they saw him no more. But still they stood gazing upward, hoping to catch one more glimpse of their departing Lord. Then two angels came and stood beside them, clothed in beautiful garments of white. They said, "Men of Galilee, why do you stand gazing up into heaven? This same Jesus who is taken up from you into heaven will come again in the same manner as he went away."

Then they left the place and went into Jerusalem, into a room upstairs, where they met together with other friends of Jesus to wait and pray until the promised Comforter should be given to them. No longer were they sorrowing; for now great joy filled their hearts because they knew that Jesus was really the Christ.

ELSIE E. EGERMEIER (1890–1986) was born on a farm in Sanborn, Iowa. Educated in rural schools in Iowa, Tennessee, and Oklahoma, she went to work as a copywriter for Gospel Trumpet Co. publishing company in 1909. Two years later, in 1911, she became an editor of juvenile fiction. Egermeier wrote many religious stories for young people. Her *Egermeier's Bible Story Book*, excerpts of which are published here, sold over a million copies before the first revision in 1955.